# WEET'S QUEST

# WEET'S QUEST

## BY JOHN WILSON

### ILLUSTRATIONS BY JANICE ARMSTRONG

Napoleon Publishing

Cover art:    Alan Barnard
Book design:  Craig McConnell


Napoleon & Company
Toronto, Ontario, Canada


Printed in Canada
Second printing 2007


12 11 10 09 08 07   5 4 3 2


Canadian Cataloguing in Publication Data

Wilson, John (John Alexander), 1951-
        Weet's quest

ISBN  0-929141-52-0

I. Title.

PS8595.I5834W4   1997          jC813'.54 C97-931446-1
PZ7.W54We   1997

For Jeni -
*J. A. W.*

# CHAPTER 1

## dreams within dreams

Eric was riding on the back of a diplodocus. This was strange for several reasons. Firstly, this dinosaur lived 140 million years ago at the end of the Jurassic Period and that was 75 million years before the Late Cretaceous Period where Eric's passionate interests lay. Secondly, the diplodocus was sporting an unlikely yellow skin covered with giraffe-like black blotches. Thirdly, it was lumbering down the middle of the Eighth Avenue pedestrian precinct in Calgary.

Eric was in a saddle perched on top of the huge back and he held a set of reins which stretched forward to a tiny head over twenty feet away. By tugging on a rein, he could tell his mount to turn left or right and by pulling on both, he could bring it to a stop. The problem was, because of the length of neck, or perhaps because of the small brain at the end of it, there was a considerable delay between Eric giving a command and the creature responding.

This would not have been a worry on the open prairie, but it was a distinct disadvantage on the streets of Calgary. Already, they had done severe damage trying to take the corner around The Hudson's Bay Company and now they were systematically destroying Eighth Avenue. They were not turning any corners, but the sound of shattering glass behind them indicated that the 30 feet of waving tail was creating its own havoc with the storefronts.

Eric didn't think his parents were going to like seeing the bill for the damage. It must be in the millions by now, and they still had a long way to go to the zoo, which was the only place Eric could think of that might want a fully grown diplodocus. They were just preparing to negotiate the turn onto Centre Street when Eric spotted his sister Rose. She was hanging out of a third floor window of an office building and she was shouting something. All he could hear was the word "danger."

"What?" he yelled back. "What danger?"

"You're in danger," repeated Rose. "Watch out for the tyrannosaurus."

Eric relaxed. Rose didn't know much about dinosaurs.

"Don't be silly," he shouted. "Tyrannosaurus lived at the end of the Cretaceous. This is the Jurassic. Diplodocus and tyrannosaurus never met."

Even as he corrected her, Eric felt uneasy. After all, no diplodocus had ever walked the streets of

Calgary either. However, he had no time to draw the obvious conclusion before a tyrannosaurus emerged from the McLeod Trail underpass. Looking like an unearthly 10 ton ostrich, the beast pivoted on its three splayed toes and looked at Eric. The eyes were set on the front of the face above deep red slashes of colour which extended back to the bulging neck muscles. They were obviously gauging the distance between mouth and lunch. With barely a moment's hesitation, the tyrannosaurus broke into a fast, loping run, straight at Eric.

Eric began yanking madly on the reins. It was no use. The diplodocus plodded along, apparently oblivious to the rapidly approaching danger. With one final bound, the tyrannosaurus leapt onto the diplodocus' back. As the impressive jaws loomed towards him, Eric could hear Rose shouting, "I told you so, I told you so!"

"It's all right," Eric muttered, "it's only a dream."

The tyrannosaurus had him now, shaking his shoulders and shouting, "I told you so," over and over again.

"Come on Eric, wake up," it added as Eric struggled to emerge from his nightmare. Opening one eye, he was greeted with the vision of Rose sitting on his chest and shouting excitedly, "I told you the sun would be shining. There's no stupid snow. We're going to visit Gran. Hurry up."

The diplodocus and the ruins of Calgary wavered and vanished. Reality reasserted itself. It was the first day of their Christmas holidays and they were heading out to Vancouver to stay with their Grandmother. That meant they could go skiing up at Whistler mountain, and that explained Rose's excitement. She loved skiing. In fact, Rose loved any form of speed. She was always asking their Dad to drive faster and, when they went skiing, she was always asking their Mom to allow her up onto ever steeper slopes.

The prospect of skiing explained Rose's excitement, but Eric only had himself to blame for the rude awakening. The evening before, he had taken pleasure in teasing Rose by saying that a snowstorm would close the highway and prevent them from travelling over the mountains. He had done such a convincing job that there had been tears and adult intervention had been required to calm the sobbing Rose before she would go to sleep. Eric had felt remorse then, but now, with an exuberant Rose bouncing on his chest, that had vanished.

"Get off," he groaned as he rolled from side to side in an attempt to dislodge his sister. "If you let me get up, we'll get going sooner."

Rose leapt off, jumped over Eric's scattered clothes and ski equipment and bounced across the room. At the door, she stopped and turned back. "You were dreaming about your dinosaurs again, weren't you?" she asked.

Eric nodded and waited for the inevitable comment about big lizards or things that had been dead too long. But Rose, as always, surprised him. She simply looked at him thoughtfully for a minute before slipping silently out the door.

Eric was still gazing at the door when it flew open again and a ski mitt arrowed across the room and hit him on the side of the head. "Hurry up," echoed after it as the door slammed shut and Rose's feet pounded down the stairs.

Eric yawned and swung his feet onto the floor. Sally, seeing the feet descend in front of her nose, figured it was safe and crawled out from under the bed.

"Good morning, old girl." Eric stretched down and scratched the brown hair behind the dog's right ear. "Rude way to get woken up, eh?"

Sally tilted her head into the scratch and looked up at Eric.

"But I suppose Rose is right, we'd better get up. At least we're going to see Gran. You won't have much fun stuck in the car for a couple of days, but I promise I'll take you for a nice long walk by the ocean when we get to Vancouver. Even if it's raining."

Sally looked hopeful at the sound of her favourite word and trotted around happily after Eric as he packed, dressed, and made his way downstairs.

# CHAPTER 2

*setting off*

**B**reakfast was a nightmare. Rose was a picture of noisy, perpetual motion, the adults were busy trying to ensure that the car was properly packed and that nothing important was forgotten, and Sally was excitedly getting under everyone's feet.

Through it all, Eric attempted to maintain his composure. Finally, everything was ready, the car was packed, the roof rack was securely fastened and piled with the Christmas presents, good-byes were said to the neighbours, and the family was buckled in. They were off.

As they headed out of town, Sally settled down and Rose began colouring a picture of Cinderella arriving at the ball. Eric watched the mountains get gradually closer and reflected that he would rather be going in the opposite direction. Partly, he had teased Rose the night before for the fun of it, but partly, he was hoping what he said was true. If there was a blizzard, Eric wouldn't have to leave Weet behind.

In the two months since his extraordinary trip back in time, Eric had thought of little else: the egg-stealing adventure, the stampede, and the tyrannosaurus attack. It was all so vivid in his mind, and yet the only tangible evidence of his experience was a collection of fragile bones entombed in the sixty-five-million-year-old rock of a hoodoo outside Drumheller.

Hardest of all for Eric was that Rose recalled nothing. He was so reluctant to believe that she really did not share any of his clear, sharp remembrances that he had tried several times to bring the subject up and jog her memory. But she gave him such a hard time about his dinosaur dreams that he no longer even mentioned it. He was convinced she wasn't teasing him; Rose couldn't keep a secret for ten minutes, let alone two months.

But why he could remember and she couldn't was a mystery. But then, the whole experience was a mystery, an impossible mystery. How was time travel possible?

Obviously, there had to be at least two gateways, one through the hoodoo which had taken them there and another beneath the tree at Weet's home which had put them back in the car on the way to the hoodoos. Yet these gateways were not open all the time, otherwise there would be people all over the Late Cretaceous and dinosaurs walking down Calgary streets.

What opened them and closed them? Were they only open at certain times, or were they opened by something Eric, or Rose or Sally did or said or felt? Or was it something that happened in Weet's world that opened them? Or was it a unique combination of all those factors? Eric had no idea. All he knew was that he wanted to go back—desperately. So desperately in fact that driving away from his adventure was painful.

Eric was convinced that the adventure had not been a dream. How else could he have learned about Rose's birthday present? And it hadn't felt like a dream. Dreams were like last night's ride on a diplodocus through Calgary. Even if things seemed real while you were dreaming them, they never made sense when you woke up. But the adventure with Weet still made absolute sense and was as clear and logical as a day at school. Eric smiled to himself. It had actually been more clear and logical than a lot of days at school.

And what about the bones he had found? The palaeontologists from the Royal Tyrrell Museum in Drumheller had been excited about Eric's find of the hadrosaur and the hand. As Eric had guessed, the skull was from a maiasaura, the first one found in Alberta, but the hand bones were more of a problem.

They did not belong to any species that the palaeontologists could immediately identify. That was not to say that they believed Eric when he described what he thought they were. Eric had the sense not to mention the adventure, but the experts still scoffed politely at the idea of humanoid dinosaurs. They ascribed it to the over-active imagination of a twelve-year-old. Many dinosaurs had three-fingered hands and feet and some were very delicate and capable of grasping. They assured Eric that if the rest of the skeleton were found when they returned to excavate next summer, it would turn out to be a hitherto unknown genus of the ornithomimid or "ostrich-mimic" dinosaurs.

Eric had fallen silent at that. Either these eminent scientists, who had been his heroes so recently, were right and he was an over-imaginative dreamer, or he really had met Weet and was more of an expert than they would ever be. Perhaps he would never know, but there was one thing he could do—learn. Over the two months before this Christmas trip, Eric had read everything he could on dinosaurs, in particular the ones which had dominated the terrestrial world at the end of the Cretaceous. He spent every spare waking moment bent over a book or ferreting around in the public library. He had even managed to gain access to the University of Calgary library, where he pored over dry scientific papers.

He had read everything he could lay his hands on, from the early tales of Chinese dragon's teeth and the first accounts of monstrous bones being unearthed in Europe over a century-and-a-half ago, through the initial idea that dinosaurs were stupid, maladapted creatures, almost as ponderous as some of the papers written about them, to the recent ideas which suggested a world nearly as exciting as the one he had visited. Eric was also fascinated by the new drawings and paintings which showed the dinosaurs as the active, living creatures that he knew them to be. The only problem was that, good as the paintings were, Eric found it very easy to spot mistakes in them.

Still, it was a fascinating journey of exploration for Eric. The only problem was that he had become obsessed. His school work had suffered, his other interests had fallen by the wayside and he had given up all his other hobbies. On one occasion, he had even turned down the chance of going to see his beloved Calgary Flames play against his second favourite team from Montreal. This had prompted his Dad to call him crazy, a cry which was swiftly and gleefully taken up by Rose.

And perhaps he was crazy. Maybe this was how insanity began and maybe an insane person's delusions seemed as real to them as Eric's adventures seemed to him. It was all a little frightening, the more so because Eric was so alone with his memories. There was no one he could talk things over with, no one to reassure him that it had really happened. That was why he had so much trouble working up any enthusiasm for what was happening in this world. He sensed Weet's world continually calling to him across time. Even if it were only an insane dream, he still wanted desperately to go back. But now he was travelling west, not east. If he were to find the tunnel again, it would be in the jumbled mass of hoodoos which formed the Drumheller badlands.

"Are we nearly there yet?" Rose had finished colouring. Eric groaned, he knew what was coming next. His father sighed.

"Rose," he said, "we're not even at Banff yet. Anyway, we'll probably spend the night in Kamloops and finish the drive tomorrow."

Rose's mother was more sympathetic. "That's a beautiful picture you've done," she said. "Why don't you play with your dolls now?"

"But I've no one to play with," complained Rose.

Eric tried to disappear into his seat. "Here it comes," he thought.

"Why not ask Eric nicely," replied their mother, "I'm sure he would play with you for a while. Wouldn't you Eric?"

Eric grunted.

"Please, would you play with me," said Rose in her sweetest voice. "Just for a little while."

It wasn't fair. This always happened. It was never suggested that Rose play with Eric's dinosaur models. He always ended up having to pretend to be some tiny plastic prince who lived in the tiny plastic castle which opened up to reveal a dance floor complete with changing coloured lights. And if he complained or didn't make his prince say dumb things like, "I'm so happy with you Cinderella," Rose would fuss and somehow it would be Eric's fault. The only bit he almost enjoyed was where he got to fight the dragon. Rose admitted that this was his area of expertise and allowed him to be more realistic.

"Just for a short time, Eric," said their mother, "to keep Rose happy."

"OK," replied Eric glumly. He picked up the prince. "Here comes the evil prince to destroy the castle and carry off Cinderella to feed to his pet dragon, Igor."

"Eric!"

"Eric," his mother warned, "play properly." His father chuckled.

"All right," said Eric. He settled down to play Rose's game as the walls of the Rocky Mountains began to close in around them.

# CHAPTER 3

*escape*

Gradually, the blackness receded and the world came back into focus. The last rays of the sunset glanced off a thick branch near his face. It was peaceful just lying here, safe and protected by the foliage, but there was a nagging suspicion that there was something that needed to be done. And there was that noise. It was coming from close by and sounded like heavy breathing.

The roarer! In a rush Weet's memories came flooding back—the attack, his friends trapped by the roots of the falling tree, his attempts to whistle the roarer away. And now the roarer was hunting him. Weet froze. The breathing was coming closer, the roarer's shape loomed above him to the left, slowly searching the underbrush as it moved nearer.

The roarer probably wouldn't see Weet since its eyesight was much better at spotting movement than shapes. If he kept still it would miss him in the gathering dark. But it might smell him. Weet had to do something.

# WILSON

Running was out of the question—those jaws would have him before he took three steps. Moreover, he was so entangled in the app branches that it would be impossible to break free quickly. In fact, he was lying in a mess of squashed apps and broken twigs. Perhaps that was the answer. It was certainly his only hope.

Very slowly and very quietly, Weet reached out and pulled an app from a branch hanging in front of his face. It was soft and ripe. Squeezing hard, Weet spread the juice over himself. If he could cover himself in enough fruit juice, then that might mask his own smell from the roarer.

But he mustn't rush. Any movement could attract the roarer. Then Weet, the bush and the apps would simply disappear down that cavernous throat. The snorting was getting closer as Weet slowly covered his body with juice. He couldn't reach his legs, but he hoped there was enough squashed fruit down there already. They certainly felt wet enough.

With an extra loud snort, the roarer's head swung over Weet. He could feel the warm breath on his face and smell the overpowering odour of rotting meat from deep within the beast's throat. The snout was only about three feet above him and he could see the great curved teeth clearly against the dark mass of the head. The breath from the flared nostrils washed over Weet and rustled the leaves around him.

For what seemed like an eternity, the roarer

examined the broken branches and squashed fruit which hid Weet. Then, with agonizing slowness, it moved away. Weet closed his eyes and allowed himself to breathe.

Not until it was completely dark and he could no longer hear the snorts of the roarer did Weet dare to move out of the shattered debris of his tree ring. A terrible pain pounded away at the back of his skull where it had hit the branch, and his shoulder ached.

Eventually, the pounding subsided a little and Weet managed to drag himself out of the tangle of branches. He had been lucky, but where were the others? His family would have dispersed into the dusk—safe for now from the roarer. But Eric, Rose and Sa"y had been trapped by the falling tree.

He began to remember now that they had fallen, or been pushed by the roots, down into a hole. Perhaps it had been deep enough to protect them. Another thought struck Weet. Perhaps they were buried and suffocating under the tree roots. How long had he been unconscious?

Stumbling in the blackness, Weet felt his way over to the huge tangle of muddy roots at the bottom of the fallen tree. "Eric," he whistled softly. "Rose, Sa"y, come here."

There was no reply. Gingerly, Weet began to scoop his way through the mess. Earth coated the roots and made them slippery. Even if it had not been dark, Weet would not have been able to see much because of the dirt that fell into his eyes every time he moved. The ground between the roots was soft and Weet's feet sank into it, but there was no sign of a hole. It must have filled in. His friends were buried alive!

Frantically, Weet began digging. He didn't know if he was in the right place. He couldn't see where he was throwing the handfuls of earth he scooped up. He might even have been burying them deeper, but he had to do something. His shoulder hurt, and every time he bent over, his head felt as if it would explode. But he had to try.

These strange creatures, who had suddenly come into his world and didn't seem to know the simplest thing about living in it, had become his friends. They had saved his life and he had saved theirs. That was special. That made them almost family.

Weet would, of course, have worked till he dropped to try and save his age-mates or the hatchlings. But something else attracted him to these strangers. He couldn't explain it, but he sensed that, in some way, Eric and Rose knew more about his world than he did. It was not just Eric's strange tools and the sticks he used to make fire. It was knowledge. Not the shaky, grubby knowledge of the homs, but a deeper understanding. Somehow, these three strangers held the key to the nature of Weet's world. He had to rescue them.

But all his efforts were in vain. No sooner did he start a hole than the soft earth would cave back in. Or else he would hit a buried root. If the falling tree had pushed his friends back out of the hole, the roarer would have eaten them. If they were buried, they were buried so deep that he would never be able to dig them out. Either way, they were lost.

Weet slumped back exhausted against a muddy root. His friends were gone. The adventures of the last few days were over. Oh, he would find his family and they would move to another home and raise the baby shovelbill and have a normal life again. But Weet would never know where his friends had come from. Perhaps worst of all, for the rest of his life he would live with an aching loneliness that no one else would understand.

A rustling in the darkness interrupted Weet's thoughts. His first idea was that the roarer had returned, but the noise was too small and close. As he strained to hear, a familiar shape nestled in against his outstretched leg.

"Sinor," Weet sighed as his hand slid down to caress his pet's head. "You understand. You have lost a friend too."

The last thought that crossed Weet's mind before he drifted off into a fitful sleep was that he must at least try to learn some of the things that Eric, Rose and Sa"y knew. He didn't know where to start, but he would think of something and he would never give up trying.

# CHAPTER 4

## *the accident*

"Are we nearly there yet?" It was dark now, even though it was only late afternoon. A ghostly full moon cast a pale light over the landscape. By Eric's count, that was the fifteenth time Rose had asked that question.

"Not too long now," their father replied. "We've made good time. Another hour or so should get us to Kamloops. Keep an eye out for a motel."

Eric looked out the window of the car. It didn't look like promising motel country. On his left the dark shapes of trees marched past at high speed. To his right, on the other side of a deep ditch, was a crumbling rock wall, so close at times that it seemed blurred. The road was winding and the car's headlights lit the piles of dirty snow which lay ahead on the road's shoulders.

Eric's father was right, they had made good time, but it had still been a long day. Sally had slept through most of it, curled on the seat beside Eric. Rose, however, was not a good car traveller. She didn't like sitting in one place for a long time, and Rose considered anything more than ten minutes a long time. Eric had done his best, playing card games and princesses and dragons, but now everyone was getting tired.

"I'm hungry. When are we going to eat?" This was Rose's second most popular question and it was one that Eric was beginning to sympathize with.

"As soon as we get to Kamloops," their mother replied, "we'll find a restaurant and have supper."

"But I'm hungry now. I can't wait another hour."

"Rose, we're going as fast as we can. If you're really hungry, have a piece of fruit from the bag."

Rose glumly picked an apple out and took a bite.

"Yecch, it's sour," she said, dropping it back on the floor.

"Pick it up, please," said their mother in a voice that hinted at the lecture on tidiness to come. But Eric wasn't listening. Rose's words had whisked him back 65 million years to another time when his sister had uttered those very words.

Why couldn't she remember the strange fruit Weet had offered them? Eric was confused. He was sorry Rose couldn't remember their adventures, but he was also angry at her for leaving him so alone with his thoughts. He would have given anything for her to remember and to be able to talk about all they had experienced.

What was Weet doing now? Eric knew that was a silly question. Weet was a collection of fossil bones now, but he couldn't help thinking of Weet's time and his own as running parallel. Then an interesting thought struck him. Supposing time in their two worlds was running parallel in some bizarre way, did time have to move at the same speed in both worlds? Eric had been in Weet's world for three whole days and yet he had not been gone from his own for any time at all. In fact, he had come back earlier than he had left. Perhaps years were passing in Weet's world while he sat trapped for hours in this car.

Eric remembered a story he had once read in which time was continually splitting into different realities. For example, there would be a world where Lee Harvey Oswald's bullets had missed President Kennedy. Eric's world and the alternative one would be the same up to that point, but from then on things would be very different as the consequences of Kennedy's continuing to be president of the United States would begin to pile up.

Perhaps in that world there would have been no war in Vietnam. One minor consequence of that would have been that Jim Petrie's parents would not have moved up to Canada to avoid the draft and Jim would not now be in Eric's grade at school. Perhaps in that world, Jim would not even have been born. That would mean that he could not have pushed Eric off the monkey bars in grade four and Eric would not now have that long scar on his left leg.

The assumption in the story had been that all the time lines moved at the same speed. But what if they didn't and the present in Eric's world corresponded with the Roman Empire or the Age of Fishes somewhere else? Then it was also possible for it to correspond to the Late Cretaceous of Weet's world.

Another possibility was that the time lines didn't run parallel and were intertwined like the fibres in a huge piece of rope. Then the lines might get caught up and perhaps two could somehow merge and allow travel from one to the other. Or perhaps the lines could get tangled into huge knots and it would be possible to travel into a different piece of your own time line.

Eric was just guessing, but he had always doubted that time was a constant. Whenever he got scared, for instance, time would slow down. Eric remembered that time when he had fallen from the monkey bars. After Jim Petrie's shove, he had seemed to spend an age waving his arms and trying vainly to regain his balance. And the fall, although it was only about eight feet, had seemed to last forever. Eric could still remember watching the world from strange angles as he tumbled to the earth and having time to think, "How odd the playground looks upside down."

On the other hand, whenever he was doing

something he really enjoyed, like reading when he should be asleep, time seemed to fly by. Maybe whole worlds could speed up and slow down! Who could know for sure?

"So with all this stuff in the car we have to be tidy, OK, Rose?" Eric's mother had finished her tidiness lecture.

"Ok, Mom," Rose mumbled. Eric was afraid this would precede another round of princesses and dragons, but Rose lapsed into silence and gazed disconsolately at the eerily-lit scenery.

Eric peered ahead at the snow, which reminded him of a picture he had seen recently. Of course, it had been of a dinosaur—he had looked at little else for weeks—but this one stood out. It had been of a tyrannosaur standing alone, pivoting on its massive hind legs, and reaching down to drink from a pond or river. What had caught Eric's attention had been the fact that the dinosaur had broken through a skim of ice to get at the water. In addition, a thin powdering of snow lay around its feet.

Dinosaurs in snow—that was a radical idea. The only place it would have been possible was very close to the poles. Sixty-five million years ago, Eric's beloved dinosaur hunting grounds in southern Alberta would have been just north of 60 degrees latitude. That was equivalent to the present day Northwest Territories, but the Cretaceous climate had been much warmer and the Alberta monsters had lived in a warm, almost sub-tropical, world and experienced only minor seasonal variations.

But Eric knew that dinosaurs had ranged much farther north than Alberta. Their remains had been found in Alaska and the Yukon, very close to the Cretaceous north pole. This presented problems for those scientists who believed dinosaurs were cold-blooded. Even though the climate had been much warmer, the very high latitudes had still been subject to a long polar night when temperatures dropped enough to kill cold-blooded animals too large to hibernate.

One proposed solution had the dinosaurs migrating south each year in vast herds, much like the caribou did now. But there was another problem—the distances involved were immense. The round trip from the Yukon to Alberta was thousands of miles. To do it every year would have required several times the annual energy available to a large, cold-blooded animal and therefore was clearly impossible. A cold-blooded, three-ton hadrosaur would not have been able to eat enough to supply the energy needed to move his bulk that far every year.

If large dinosaurs had lived in the Arctic, they must have been warm-blooded. Eric could see no way around it. There was also the evidence of his own eyes, which had seen the high level of activity in the dinosaurs. This activity must have meant they were warm-blooded.

So it wasn't the cold in Weet's world that was making them sick. Weet had been wrong. Perhaps the cold was making them susceptible to disease or perhaps the cold was unrelated. Eric had read one theory which said that sickness carried by dinosaurs migrating from Asia to America had been a factor in their decline.

If only Eric could go back to look for more clues. It was all so frustrating. He tried to imagine what Weet was doing. Was he still with his family? Had they found another home? Was Weet training the hadrosaur, the one he called a shovelbill?

Eric looked around. Rose was asleep beside him. At least it was quiet and peaceful now. He was pulled out of his reverie by approaching headlights. Judging by their height they must belong to a semi-trailer. And they were bright. Too bright. The road curved gently around the mountainside to the right and there didn't seem to be enough room for their car to pass the truck. Eric sat up and stared ahead.

"He's on the wrong side . . ." There was panic in his mother's voice. The lights were blinding now and horribly close.

"Move over!" Eric's Dad was yelling frantically at the approaching danger. As if to prove the point Eric had been thinking about earlier, things began to slow down. The car jerked and skidded in slow motion as Eric's father stood on the brakes. The lights were almost on them now and the air was filled with the booming sound of the truck's horn. Eric found himself willing the car to speed up, but the car wasn't listening. It seemed to be sliding sideways now in an almost leisurely fashion. The truck's wheels appeared very big to Eric.

Rose was sitting up now, too.

"What?" was all she had time to say before the world exploded. With almost detached interest, Eric felt the shock of the crash. He felt the seat belt cut into him as he was thrown forward. He felt the rush of cold air as the windscreen disintegrated. Pieces of glass were flying everywhere. Rose's half-eaten apple flew past his face and out the broken window. Rose screamed. Sally barked. Metal screeched in protest as it was torn apart. Above it all, the truck's horn continued its mournful chorus.

Then everything went black and very quiet.

# CHAPTER 5

*Weet's quest*

**W**eet surveyed the valley below as the early morning sun chased the shadows across its floor. The valley had changed since the homs left. The barren slopes were clothed in a new green carpet, although there were still ragged brown streaks of erosion scarring its sides. The circular site of the village in the curve of the river seemed slower to regenerate than the rest.

It had been almost three years since the adventure here with Eric, Rose and Sa"y and Weet often came back to remember. In the early days, he had gone down to sit and reflect in the ruins of the hom village, but there was nothing there for him and he found the desolation depressing. Now he just sat on the valley rim and remembered.

He remembered the adventures, the frightening times and the funny times. He remembered the roarer attack and his friends' disappearance as if it were yesterday. It had been only three days in his life yet he had not been the same since. In an attempt to find out what Eric knew, Weet had become almost obsessed with discovery. Nothing happened that he did not think about or study.

He had trained the baby shovelbill to become the mount he rode today. He had tried to make second skins from the feathers of the sickleclaw but had discovered that shredding and tying the strands of nan creeper produced an equally effective insulator from the cold. He was wearing a simple sleeveless jacket of this material now.

He had also studied all the sick shovelbills he had come across to see if he could figure out what was causing their illness. At first, he had assumed it was the cold that was making the animals sick, but in time, he began to think there was some other cause. They were warm to the touch even when they were in the last stages of illness. In fact, they often seemed considerably warmer when they were really sick.

And then there were the borers. These small red insects seemed to make their home by digging themselves under the tough skins of the shovelbills. If they were left alone, they quickly formed hard lumps under the skin which would burst and release a horde of tiny, flying beetles. Weet assumed that the beetles would then go and lay eggs which would hatch into the red insects and the cycle would be repeated. All the shovelbills seemed to have them, but there were often a very large number of them on the sick animals. Even his own mount had them, although Weet dug them out whenever he saw them. He had to be quick, because the whole boring and hatching process under the shovelbill's skin could happen in just a few hours.

Was this the cause of the sickness? If so, why didn't all the shovelbills get sick and die? Perhaps there had to be a lot of the bugs, or perhaps some shovelbills were immune. Certainly, Weet's mount never seemed to get sick although it always seemed to have some borers. It was very confusing.

Weet wished he could talk to Eric. He probably could still talk to him quite well even now. He could remember all the words he had learned of Eric's language and several that he did not know the meaning of. Despite the fact that he had no one to talk to and no hope of ever seeing Eric again, he practised speaking, mainly to his always curious but uncommunicative pet Sinor.

Of all Weet's experiments, the most frustrating had been his efforts to make fire. At first, he had tried to collect fire from the smouldering hom village and then from nearby lightning strikes, but each time he had not been able to keep the flame alive. He understood now the advantage the homs had in living in villages with many fires always burning. Even if most of them went out, they could always be rekindled from the remaining ones.

Underlying all Weet's activity, there was a

restlessness. Certainly he was learning things and perhaps one day he would even solve the problem of fire, but he had a strong feeling that he was not dealing with the root of the problems which faced his world. Weet needed something radical to happen, but what?

Beneath him the shovelbill shifted restlessly. A small group of them was moving along the distant river bank. It was almost hatching season and Weet's mount wanted to join the herd heading for the coastal nesting sites. Weet had no trouble keeping the placid beast under control with gentle tugs on the reins, but he too was beginning to feel restless. All his people would be gathering for the nesting soon. Weet had delayed, but this time he would have to find a partner and move off to establish his own family.

His parents had tolerated his thoughtfulness, even though all his age-mates had already moved out and set up families, but he knew they wouldn't any longer. This year he would have to go. Then he would have to spend his time and energy on finding a tree circle and raising hatchlings. There would be precious little time for observing and thinking.

But he knew he had to keep learning if he had any hope of discovering what Eric had known. Sadly, Weet turned the reluctant shovelbill back to his tree circle.

He arrived back for a communal breakfast and

conversation about the upcoming hatching. Since the last of his age mates had left, Weet had found himself becoming increasingly quiet. This morning, however, he was even more preoccupied than usual. After the last of the fruit was passed around, Weet wandered out of the tree ring to gaze westward where the land rose gently to the distant peaks of the young Rocky Mountains.

He was particularly restless this morning, as if every muscle in his body was charged with electricity and wouldn't let him sit still or relax. But he had no idea what he could do to stop it. All he knew was that he would have to do something.

A soft morning breeze gently rustled the leaves of the bushes around his feet. Nearby, the shovelbills browsed on some low bushes. Overhead a large V-formation of ters was heading west, their broad wings flapping in a slow, stately rhythm. They would be heading out to the great ocean over the mountains, where they nested on islands. The germ of an idea began to form in Weet's mind. Turning abruptly, he hurried back into the tree ring in search of his father.

"Tell me the story of the origin," he whistled.

His father looked sideways at his son and Weet longed for the funny facial movements through which Eric and Rose communicated how they felt.

"If you wish," his father replied. "We have not always lived here. Long ago, uncountable hatchings before you were born, our people lived far away, over the mountains. We had a good life, beside the great water. There was abundant food, fish and shells from the water and fruit and roots from the earth. It was safe in the forests of giant trees and the few roarers were smaller than the ones here and preferred to hunt shovelbills on the river plains or crestnecks on the uplands. It was a perfect world and we had many hatchlings each season.

"But then the first sickleclaws came. They came from the cold, following the edge of the water. They were smaller than the sickleclaws here and moved easily through the trees where we lived. At that time, we had not learned how to whistle them and they found us easier prey than the larger animals of the open. They were very fast and silent and we lost many young to them.

"Some of us tried to adapt by living in the trees, but most stuck to the old ways and gradually we became fewer and fewer. One terrible year, the sickleclaws attacked the hatching. The stories say that there were hundreds of them and that it was a slaughter. They were killing for the fun of it because they could not possibly eat all that they caught.

"Eventually, a band who had lost everything was forced away from the water and began the epic journey that brought us here. They were led by one called Weet and his mate. He led them away from the danger and pointed them towards our new land. We owe him all that we have.

"Sadly, when the band was passing near Fire Mountain, disaster struck. The mountain exploded, the band was broken up and Weet, along with many others, perished. But his mate survived and she was carrying eggs. Every year at the hatching, we name some of those descended from her eggs 'Weet' in honour of our saviour. You are such a one.

"The few survivors of the trek eventually found a habitable land. It was not the paradise they had left, but it was manageable and, by the time the sickleclaws arrived, they had learned the effect of whistling and were safe."

Weet's father stopped whistling and gazed fixedly at his son.

"Has anyone ever gone back?" Weet asked.

"No," came the reply, "it is too dangerous."

"But," Weet continued, "now that we can whistle, we need not fear the sickleclaws. If the land really was paradise, we could make it ours again."

"It is too dangerous," his father repeated. "It is impossible to pass Fire Mountain and, even if one could, the sickleclaws over there are different. Here they hunt alone or in groups of four or five. When they attacked the hatching so many years ago, there were many of them. I'm not sure that even our whistling would have stopped them."

"I'm going," said Weet simply. He had not planned to be so direct. In fact, until the words were out, he had not been sure what he wanted. But now he felt that he had to leave. He had to learn and there was nothing that he could be taught staying here.

Over there, where it was different, where his people had come from, perhaps there would be clues that would tell him something. If he learned about the past, that might show him something about the future. In any case, it was all he could think of doing. Eric was gone and the homs had failed. At the very least, the adventure of the journey would take his mind off the horrible loneliness he felt gnawing at the pit of his stomach.

His father regarded Weet with his fixed, unchanging stare. It was a strange decision, but then Weet was the strangest of his hatchlings. He had proved it by getting the egg and raising the shovelbill. In any case, he would be leaving the family at the next hatching. He cupped his hands in a gesture of acceptance, love, and farewell.

Weet nodded and cupped his hands in reply. There was no point in delaying.

Turning, Weet cupped his hands in farewell to his mother and the hatchlings. A flurry of cupped hands answered his gesture. There was no regret or remorse on his side, for the decision had been made. With Sinor at his heels, he walked out of the tree ring that had been his home since the great adventure with Eric, Rose and Sa"y. With only the briefest of backward glances, Weet mounted the shovelbill and set off westwards, toward the dry hills and Fire Mountain.

# CHAPTER 6

### *back again*

Gradually, Eric moved toward the light. At least he seemed to, but the light was not getting any brighter. And it was getting uncomfortably hot. He was sitting against something rough and hard and a weight lay across his knees.

"Strange," he thought dully. "Where am I?"

"Open your eyes and look around," suggested Eric's sluggish brain.

"Good idea," replied Eric. "Maybe Rose knows what's going on."

Eric opened his eyes. Then he hurriedly closed them again. It was not the brightness or the sight of an unconscious Rose draped across his legs that made him shut out the scene before him. It was the sight of two sets of the largest toenails imaginable.

"I must be hallucinating," thought Eric. "Perhaps if I start by looking up."

Eric tilted his head back and tried raising his eyelids once more. This was more promising. Above him hung the tree against which his back was resting. It seemed immensely tall from this position, soaring far up into the sky, where huge branches reached out from the trunk. As Eric watched, a branch above his head reached over and took a mouthful of foliage.

With a start, Eric jerked forward. His eyes slid unwillingly down the huge neck, over the massive shoulders and chest to the two pillar-like legs planted firmly on the ground not ten feet in front of him. There, once more, were the nightmarish toenails.

Eric let out a short whimper. "Rose," he whispered urgently to the inert form lying across his legs. There was no response. Looking around, he saw Sally lying beside him. She was panting and beginning to move. He looked back at the unearthly toenails. The beast hadn't noticed him, but he would hate to get stepped on by mistake. On the other hand, if he moved away, he risked attracting some unwelcome attention.

Eric had almost decided to remain where he was and keep very still when the feet rose to hang threateningly in the air above his head. Frantically clutching Rose, he dragged her around the tree into the open. Unfortunately, the view was no more reassuring there. Eric had only taken three or four steps when he froze. The close-up of the toenails had been bad enough, but the rest of the creature was even more awesome.

"I'm back!" was the next thought that crossed his mind. "But back where?"

The three travellers were in the middle of a broad, undulating plain. It had a moderate slope and supported some of the largest trees Eric had ever seen. Some stood in splendid isolation. Others, like the one beside him, were part of widely-spaced clumps. The ground between was covered with low ferns, although occasional bushes with broad leaves, and even rare flowers, were scattered about. The trees were evergreens of some sort—firs Eric guessed. The lower reaches of the trees were bare, but, above that, thick branches covered in coarse, dark green needles, grew straight out from the trunk.

Many of the trees were well over 100 feet high, but it was not their immensity that held the stunned Eric's attention. It was the creatures who were lunching on them. The beast he was attempting to escape was obviously not alone. Almost every tree and cluster provided grazing for a herd of the strangest animals Eric had ever seen. They resembled vast snakes which had each swallowed an elephant. Four trunk-like legs supported a massive body—this was the elephant part. The snake part consisted of a long neck on which was perched a small, yet robust-looking, head. An equivalent length of tail stretched out behind. A row of spines began at the back of the head and extended the entire length of the back, the rest of which appeared to be covered with scales of various sizes. Most of the creatures were standing on all four legs, placidly munching on the lower branches. Even this way, they had no difficulty reaching up twenty or even thirty feet. However some, including the one they had already been introduced too, were balancing on their hind legs and tail and stretching up to even higher branches.

"Dragons," whispered the emotional part of Eric's brain. "No, sauropods," whispered back the logical part.

Eric's mind was reeling. He was looking at—no, he was in the middle of—a herd of grazing sauropod dinosaurs. According to the scientific experts, no human being had any business being part of this picture, but the significance of it was lost on the dinosaurs who continued filling their vast stomachs and completely ignored the puny intruders into their ancient world.

Slowly, Eric half-carried, half-dragged the unconscious Rose over to a tree on the far side of the clump. Sally, awake by now, trotted after the pair.

The conversation in Eric's head continued.

"Well," said the logical part in a superior voice, "obviously, you are back in time again."

"All very well," his emotions responded with just a touch of panic, "but where and when?"

"Ok then, let's think this through," came the reply. "The last time we arrived in the late Cretaceous. That was when the rocks we were crawling through at the time were deposited. Is that a rule of time travel, I wonder?"

"There are no rules of time travel!" A note of near hysteria was creeping into the emotional side of the conversation. "Time travel is impossible!"

"It would appear not," came the rational reply. "Now, keep quiet and let me think. What age are the rocks around Kamloops? Older than Cretaceous, I think. Perhaps Jurassic. That would explain the sauropod dinosaurs. They dominated the Jurassic Period around 140 million years ago."

"Why would we have gone back to the Jurassic?" interrupted the other half as a sudden wave of sadness swept over Eric. And then, "If this is the Jurassic," he thought, "I'll never see Weet again."

"Right," continued his intelligence, "the Jurassic was 75 million years before Weet."

"Shut up!" said Eric out loud.

"What?" Rose was awake and looking groggily around. "We're back!" she said in a stunned voice as she took in the extraordinary scene.

"Back?" Eric turned to his sister. "Then you remember?"

"Of course I do!" Rose frowned at Eric. "How did you think I could forget?"

Eric hugged his sister. She remembered! He wasn't alone anymore and he wasn't crazy.

"Get off!" said Rose, pushing him away. "What's the matter with you?"

"You remember Weet, the homs, the tyrannosaurus?"

"Yes, why shouldn't I?" There was an edge of petulance creeping into Rose's voice. But she looked puzzled.

"You didn't remember when we were back in our world," Eric explained. "I felt so lonely. That's why I hugged you just now."

"But I remember now," said Rose, brushing off Eric's emotional outburst. She stopped and looked around. "We're back, but where, and how did we get here?"

In a moment all the horror of the car crash came back to Eric—the lights, the screams, the sound of tearing metal, the truck's insistent horn. No one could have survived that impact. Were they dead? Where were their parents? Had they somehow miraculously survived? Maybe they had all been killed, but Eric, Rose and Sally had time-jumped at the last second. Maybe they would be stuck here forever. Maybe they would return to find their parents dead. Eric shuddered and glanced over at his sister. How much did she remember?

"There was a car crash," he said, as casually as he could manage. "We must have bumped our heads."

Rose looked confused. "I don't remember . . ." she began. "I was dozing and I dreamt I heard a strange sound. Then I woke up here."

"We were just looking for a motel," Eric explained. "We had to swerve to avoid a truck. We must have banged our heads."

Eric deliberately played down the crash. If Rose didn't remember, there was no point in upsetting her.

"Where are we?" Rose looked up.

"I'm not sure," replied Eric. Then he added rather unhelpfully, "We were heading for Kamloops when we crashed."

"But we're in Weet's time?" Rose turned to her brother with a worried look on her face.

"I don't know," replied Eric. "Toenails here is a sauropod dinosaur and they were common in the Jurassic Period almost 75 million years before Weet."

"No!" The violence of Rose's exclamation took Eric by surprise. He looked apprehensively at the grazing dinosaurs, but they paid no attention. "We must be in Weet's time!"

"Look," continued Eric, "I have no idea how this time travel stuff works but, even if we are in the late Cretaceous, there is no guarantee that we're in exactly the same time. We could be just a couple of million years out and, even if we are exactly right in time, we're obviously in a different place so the chances of finding Weet are pretty slim."

As soon as he finished speaking, Eric knew he had made a mistake. Rose's eyes were filling up with tears. He should have shut up or reassured her that they might well meet Weet and everything would be all right. Rose's mood swung over into anger.

"You always spoil everything. Why do you have to be like that? You don't know how we got here or where we are any more than I do. I think we came here to see Weet again and we will!" Abruptly, Rose stormed away from the tree.

"Rose!" Eric shouted. "Come back!"

As if in response to his cry, the closest dinosaur dropped back to the ground with the force of a small earthquake. Across the hillside, other animals were doing the same. Rose stopped running. Something was wrong. The herd had stopped eating and was cautiously sniffing the air, looking around, and calling to one another. As Eric watched, all the animals began moving together along the hillside.

"Rose, get back here!" This time his sister paid attention to his call and scuttled back to his side. Sally huddled at his feet. The sauropods were stampeding, but it was a stampede in slow motion.

The fastest only moved at the pace of a brisk walk. But several hundred tons of moving dinosaur throws up a thick cloud of dust. The trio pressed themselves against the tree trunk and hoped for the best.

Around them, the slow-motion chaos continued. The dust thickened until Eric could not see more than a few feet in any direction. Their world closed into a swirling mass of stifling heat, choking dust and thundering footsteps. The small group sat, sweated, and waited for the worst to pass.

Eventually the thundering eased off and Eric ventured to open an eye. The dust still swirled around them, but it was thinning slightly. The sound of massive footsteps had died down. Deciding it was time to move, and safest to do it in the opposite direction from the stampede, Eric grabbed Rose by the hand and stepped around the tree. That was when he saw the head.

It seemed to hover in the dust-laden air at the level of Eric's face and only about three feet away. It was very large, but surprisingly narrow. The jaws were slightly open and revealed a set of very large teeth. Above them a pair of dark nostrils flared inquisitively and two perfectly round eyes regarded Eric with curiosity. Above the eyes, two short, blunt horns stood straight up. Eric had the uncomfortable feeling that the interest in the eyes was culinary.

"Albertosaurus," said the logical part of his mind. "Not as large as tyrannosaurus—only about three or four tons in weight—but a fearsome predator nonetheless. Probably hunted in packs. Definitely Late Cretaceous, so the sauropods must be a remnant which survived long after the main families died out."

The emotional part of Eric's mind screamed. So did Rose. Sally let out a low growl. The huge eyes blinked. Eric stood paralyzed, hypnotized by those eyes and those teeth. He wondered what it would be like to be swallowed by an Albertosaurus.

The head swung down and tilted curiously. The jaws opened farther. Eric gulped nervously. Time was certainly moving slowly now, but he wished it would speed up or that he could take advantage of the slow motion to run away. The teeth were now very close. Eric had an insane desire to reach out and feel how sharp they were. Would it be less painful to be chewed up or swallowed whole?

Eric's speculations were interrupted by three events in quick succession. He heard a loud crack, followed immediately by a long swishing sound. He felt a rush of air against his cheek. He saw a wide, red gash open almost magically in the Albertosaurus' shoulder. The beast roared deafeningly and staggered to the side.

Before it could recover, a shadow loomed above the cowering children's heads. A pair of jaws appeared. They were much less impressive than the ones Eric had just faced, but were obviously strong and carried a battery of peg-like teeth. The teeth fastened onto the Albertosaurus' neck. The predator roared in pain and jerked its head in a vain attempt to shake off its attacker. Eventually, the jaws relaxed their grip and the Albertosaurus, bleeding from the gash in its shoulder and its neck wound, staggered off down the hillside. Twitching its long tail triumphantly, the sauropod watched the beast's retreat before tramping on its way to join the rest of the herd.

Eric let out a breath he had been holding for a painfully long time.

"Thanks, toenails," he mumbled to the disappearing monster. "Are you OK, Rose?"

"Yes," came the rather weak reply. "What was that?"

"My guess would be a Titanosaurid," replied Eric. "They were a Late Cretaceous family of sauropods that lived in the American west. No one has ever found one this far north, but then we are in a very different environment from Alberta." Eric chuckled. "So much for the idea that they were dumb and slow. That guy could sure fight, and he saved our lives. That tail was so fast we didn't even

see it. Did you see how strong the neck was to hold onto an angry Albertosaurus?"

But Rose was thinking of something else.

"So if this is the Late Cret...aceous," she said thoughtfully, "we could be in Weet's time?"

"Yes," Eric admitted, "we could be."

"Well then," said Rose, getting up purposefully and brushing the dust off her clothes, "I guess we had better go and look for him."

In amazement, Eric watched his sister stride away from the tree and along the hillside. Her single-mindedness could shrug off the most horrifyingly narrow escape from death and keep her focused on the one thing she wanted to believe—that they would meet Weet again. Eric smiled. It felt really good to have Rose back in this adventure with him. With as light a step as he could manage on his still shaky legs, and with Sally at his heels, he followed his sister into the unknown.

# CHAPTER 7

*meeting*

For several days now, Weet had been questioning his decision to cross the mountains. It was not that the going was difficult—the mountains weren't much higher than hills, so most of the time he was riding through pleasant open country. The food was also plentiful and, although the nights were colder than down on the plain, he had had no trouble finding brush to make a comfortable bed. What was really upsetting Weet was what was in his mind.

The loneliness Weet had felt when he had realized that his friends were gone had doubled now that he had left his family behind. This surprised him because he had thought that he was prepared for leaving them. But the reality of never seeing them again—and Weet couldn't see how he ever would if he went through with his plan—was different.

He found himself thinking about them often: his father's stories, his mother's attention when he was injured, his games with his age-mates, even the cute annoyances of the hatchlings. All of this seemed much more precious now that he had left it behind. And for what? It was an impulse, not properly thought through. How would he manage alone over the mountains? What would he find when he got to the other side? Perhaps there was no one left. Perhaps his father was right and the whistling wouldn't work against the sickleclaws there. It was insane.

A couple of times he had almost turned around and gone home. No one would criticize him for it. What had stopped him was his own stubbornness and a still uncrystallized feeling that, however difficult it was, he was doing the right thing.

At least, he was fulfilling his aim of learning about his world. The higher Weet climbed, the stranger the surroundings and the inhabitants became. Most notably, there were many longnecks. They only rarely ventured down where Weet's family lived. He could only remember seeing two or three in his whole life. Now they were all around him, browsing on the tall trees and calling to each other in their odd, snorting voices. The first, close-up view of them had been scary, but in fact they were placid beasts, concentrating mostly on eating and taking almost no notice of the miniature world around their feet.

These upper slopes also had crestnecks and shovelbills, although not nearly in the same numbers as down below. Weet supposed that the reason was the abundance of tall trees the longnecks liked eating and the shortage of short ground cover that the others preferred.

Oddly, there were few sickleclaws up here. The creatures to beware of were the small roarers. These were less than half the size of the one that had destroyed Weet's home, but they still had a fearsome array of teeth and claws. Weet had seen them before, but never as many as up here. He recognized the odd, bony crests above the eyes and the butting and kicking duels they engaged in. They seemed particularly aggressive and even hunted in small packs.

Despite his growing familiarity with this new world, Weet was still cautious and the sight of the dust cloud ahead made him rein in his mount and proceed slowly. After all, he didn't want to blunder into a pack of hunting roarers.

Eventually, Weet arrived at the edge of some trees and dismounted. In front of him was a wide open area across which a herd of longnecks was stampeding. Through the swirling dust, Weet could see the occasional roarer shadowing the herd but keeping its distance from the longnecks' waving tails. He settled down to let the drama unfold before proceeding. Sinor, glad of the rest, nestled in beside him.

As Weet watched, his eyes were drawn to a minor drama being played out off to his left. A roarer was stalking a longneck straggler. Unless more roarers arrived, the longneck was not in much danger. Weet had seen how effectively they could defend themselves. He had just settled back against a tree to enjoy some fruit when he felt Sinor tense beside him.

"What's the matter, old boy?" he whistled, using one of the expressions he had learned from Eric. But Sinor didn't settle down. In fact, he picked himself up and headed off up the hillside.

Weet whistled, but Sinor ignored him and kept going. Weet watched his pet move away through the swirling dust. He wasn't too worried—Sinor was too fast to be bothered by the roarers—but he was confused by his pet's behaviour. Sinor seemed to be heading towards the solitary longneck. As Weet watched, the longneck confronted its attacker. Pivoting, it slashed at the roarer with its whip-like tail. Its aim was good and the roarer staggered back with blood pouring from a long gash in its side. Taking advantage of its success, the longneck fastened its jaws on the roarer's back and inflicted another wound. Thoroughly discouraged, the roarer retreated along the hillside and the longneck continued on its way.

Weet found the encounter interesting, but there was nothing about it to attract Sinor. By now, his pet was almost at the site of the battle and running as fast as he could. The large animals had left, but Weet could see other, smaller figures. There were three. One was in front, striding purposefully along the hillside. It was followed by two others a short way back. Weet stopped eating and stared. He recognized the cocky, independent walk of the first one and the easy companionship of the other two even though one strode upright like himself and the other walked on all fours and was covered in brown hair. Weet dropped his fruit and, forgetting that he had a shovelbill to ride, raced up the hill after Sinor.

Eric was still shaking his head in wonder at his sister when Sally left his side and ran back towards the trees.

"Sally!" he called, but the word died in his throat. The creature racing towards Sally was very familiar. Eric thought for a moment it was a different creature from the one he knew, but the way the two animals frolicked around each other soon dispelled any doubts.

"Rose," he shouted, "look!"

Rose stopped in mid-stride, turned and let out a squeal of joy.

"Sinor!" she shouted, then "Weet!" she added, looking past Eric.

Eric turned and there he was, the figure he would have given anything to see again, striding up the hill towards them. Both children set off at full speed and their combined impact bowled over their friend. The three rolled around joyfully in the dust for some minutes before being joined by a jubilant Sally and Sinor.

To anyone watching, it would have appeared a bizarre scene; five very different creatures rolling and playing together as if they had all hatched from the same egg. At last, dust-covered figures stood up to face each other.

"He"o Eric, Rose, Sa"y," said one slowly, "I am Weet."

Eric felt like exploding with joy. He was truly back. Rose and Sally were with him and here was Weet. Their friend was a lot taller, over six feet Eric guessed, and not as skinny as before, but it was definitely Weet.

"Hello Weet," said Eric. "It's good to see you again."

"Oh Weet, I love you!" Rose was less formal than her brother. Stepping forward, she hugged the tall figure around the waist. "I just knew we had come back to see you."

She was prevented from saying more by a loud roar from along the hillside. Eric suddenly remembered that there were Albertosaurs around and that one was wounded and probably not very happy. Weet was having similar thoughts. "Come," he said and led the small group back down to the waiting shovelbill.

As soon as they were safely in the trees, they beat

some of the dust off their clothes. Weet produced some fruit from a roughly-woven bag attached to the maiasaura's saddle. As Sally and Sinor continued to reacquaint themselves, the three sat down to a meal of apps and nans.

"Mmmm," moaned Rose through a mouthful of mashed fruit. "I'd forgotten how good this stuff tasted."

"That's not what you said the first time we ate it," Eric reminded her.

"That was different," replied Rose, without explaining how.

Between munches, each told the others what had happened to them since the tyrannosaurus attack on Weet's home circle. Eric, with Rose's freely offered help, told about what he had been doing since his return to his own world. But he left out the part about finding the finger bones in the hoodoo. At several points, Rose looked puzzled as if she were only just beginning to understand why Eric had done some of the things he had. Mostly though, she cheerfully contributed her own view of the world. The only bit she could not help with was the car crash.

Weet gave them an account of his three years. He repeated his father's story about his people's early days and how it had led to his quest. Eric was amazed at how good Weet's English was. It seemed he had not forgotten a single word he had heard either of them say on the last visit. Of course, there were gaps, but with signs and inspired guesswork by Eric and Rose, Weet's story came out in considerable detail. When they had all finished, they lapsed into silence. It was broken by Rose's question.

"Well, what are we going to do?" As usual, she came straight to the point.

"I go," whistled Weet pointing a long green finger to the west. "You come me?" he added hesitantly.

"Of course," replied Eric and Rose together.

Eric had not thought before he responded but, in reality, they had no other options. There was no way either of them was going to leave Weet now that they had found him again. They both felt, as Weet did, that in some mysterious way, their fates were linked together in this strange and ancient world.

"We were heading that way anyway," Eric added flippantly.

# CHAPTER 8

## *fire mountain*

Three riders on Weet's mount made for slower progress than when Weet was alone, but no one seemed to mind. Everyone was happy to be together again. It soon felt as if they had never been apart.

All afternoon they travelled uphill through open treed country. They saw no more roarers, which pleased Eric, but passed several groups of browsing titanosaurs. There had been a minor crisis when Rose, who was sitting at the front, suddenly let out a piercing scream and fell off their mount's back. Weet had hurriedly reined the beast to a halt while Eric had jumped down. Rose was dusty but fine and looked a bit sheepish.

"What's the matter?" asked Eric.

"Bugs," replied Rose with a shiver. "Horrible red bugs."

Weet whistled a word that Eric didn't understand and pointed to the maiasaura's neck. Around a small, hard lump, there was a cluster of red insects digging into the skin.

"Not hurt," explained Weet as he picked the creatures from the maiasaura's skin and squashed them between his finger claws with a soft popping noise. As they watched, the lump seemed to move as if something were living underneath. Gingerly, Weet poked the taut skin with a finger. Gradually the skin peeled back to reveal a cluster of dark green, metallic beetles, each only about half a centimetre long. As the three watched, they opened tiny wings and took flight. Eric stepped back involuntarily, but Weet stayed where he was, busily catching the beetles between his hands.

"Yecch! What are they?" Rose had never been a fan of bugs.

"Some kind of parasite on the hadrosaur," replied Eric thoughtfully. "I doubt if they will do us any harm. They don't even seem interested in Weet."

When Rose had been coaxed back onto the maiasaura, they resumed their travels.

Around mid-afternoon, Eric noticed that they were heading towards a strange cloud. It was alone in an otherwise clear sky and was an unusual yellowish-grey colour. It appeared to billow up from behind the hill they were climbing.

By late afternoon, the cloud was looming over them and filling the view ahead. The globe of the sun, as it sank behind the cloud, turned a deep, threatening blood red colour. Eric did not regard it as a good omen. He shivered in the still warm evening air. In addition, Eric had noticed that, for the last few hours, the ground was becoming dryer, the trees were farther apart, and there were fewer animals about. There was also an odd, sharp smell in the air. No one knew what it all meant, but the strangeness made them all silently uneasy.

At last, they crested the ridge and stopped in awe. Below them, the land sloped gently away in a desert of grey dust. Not a single living thing disturbed the smooth surface of the wide valley. Nearby, some charred tree stumps poked forlornly through the dust and, farther away, shattered and twisted rocks thrust out like the desolate prows of ancient shipwrecks. The late afternoon light cast weird shadows over the bleak, colourless landscape.

To their left lay an even more extraordinary vision. The clouds they had been watching all afternoon were not clouds at all. They rose from the mountain in the distance and billowed up in huge, angry, swirling rolls to incredible heights before spreading into a vast, dirty umbrella which cast a threatening shadow over the landscape. The slopes of the mountain itself looked tortured and scarred. Deep gullies ran down the slopes, one of which led into the valley before them. The devastation of the landscape was complete. It must have been the result of an earlier cataclysm which had swept down, destroying everything in its path. The unearthly view was accompanied by low, growling rumbles interspersed with occasional sharp explosions.

Weet's mind reeled: Fire Mountain! Never had he imagined he would actually see it. He knew of the mountain from the stories and from the time the wind had blown the clouds from the mountain over his home. He had been little more than a hatchling when it had happened, but he vividly remembered his fear as the sky grew dark. He remembered the choking sensation as the dust fell and he remembered the coating on the leaves and trees. The fruit had tasted bitter for days afterwards.

But he also remembered the fun of playing with his age mates in the powdery dust and piling it into a thick layer on a nearby slope so that, when the first rains came, it turned into slippery mud which they could all slide down in messy joy. But he never thought he would stand so close to Fire Mountain.

Eric and Rose stared in silence. The view reminded Eric of the devastation he had seen the time the family took a side trip to visit Mount St. Helen's on the way home from a holiday in Oregon. But even Mount St. Helen's had been quiet when he saw it. Fire Mountain was a very large, very active volcano.

Sinor and Sally weren't thrilled with the view either. They had crested the ridge ahead of the others but, unlike their larger friends, hadn't been awed by the vast desolation. What had stopped them had been the dust itself. In only a few bouncing steps, it was up to Sinor's knees and almost over Sally's head. Amidst clouds of rising ash, which irritated their eyes and caused the pair to cough harshly, Sinor and Sally beat a hasty retreat to stand uneasily beside the maiasaura on whose broad back the three friends perched high above the dust.

"Wow," Rose said, breaking the silence.

"Yeah," agreed Eric, "we're going to have to make a wide detour around this. But not tonight," he added, looking up at the blood-red sun. "We should make sleeping mats," he said, turning to look at Weet.

"Yes," Weet agreed. "Not here."

Weet steered their mount back over the ridge and out of sight of the devastation. The slope was in shadow and there was by now a distinct chill in the air. It was going to be a cold night, especially since there was very little vegetation with which to make sleeping mats. However, they gathered what they could and made up one communal mat just large enough for them all.

"Fire?" asked Weet hopefully as they settled down.

Eric shook his head sadly. "I'm afraid not. My knife is back in the car."

"Couldn't we rub two sticks together?" Rose suggested.

"It's not as easy as that," Eric snapped, sounding harsher than he had intended. Rose didn't understand how complex things could be. "I saw a film of bushmen making fire in the Kalahari desert. It was a lot of hard work, and they were experts who knew what they were doing. What chance would we have?"

"Well, we could at least try!" Rose replied petulantly. "Your silly TV program doesn't mean we can't do it too. I'm going to try anyway."

Rose grabbed a couple of bent sticks from the mat and began furiously rubbing them together. The look of concentration on her face was so intense that Eric couldn't help but laugh.

"Careful," he chuckled, "you'll send our bed up in flames!"

Rose looked up, ready to fight, but when she saw the laughter on her brother's face, she began laughing as well.

"And we might set the volcano on fire," she gasped, doubling over as much in the relief of the day's tension as from the humour of her comment.

Weet watched this exchange between his friends with his head tilted inquisitively to one side. He didn't understand it all and he couldn't laugh, but seeing the laughter made him happier than he had been in the years since their last meeting.

"Can you make 'up in flames'?" he asked slowly.

The only response to this from Eric and Rose was a redoubling of their mirth. Eventually, Eric regained control of himself.

"OK, let's give it a try," he said and got up to go and look around the dead trees that were scattered over the slope. It didn't take him long to return with what he needed: a straight stick with a pointed end, a thick, gently curved piece of bark and some dried moss.

Sitting on the ground by the mat, he placed the bark in front of him and, using the pointed end of the stick, dug out a small hole in the middle. Placing the moss beside him, he put the pointed end of the stick in the hole and began to turn it. The easiest way was to rub his hands together with the stick between the palms. The problem was that the stick kept slipping out of his grip.

After about ten minutes he couldn't do any more and the hole in the bark was only slightly warm. Weet took over then and his long hands did a better job, but Eric was getting frustrated at the time it was taking. Then he had an idea. Searching out a bow-shaped piece of wood, Eric turned to Weet.

"Can I have a piece of vine from your bag?" he asked, accompanying his request with appropriate gestures.

Weet agreed and Eric removed a thin piece of creeper from the bag. He tied this between the ends of the bent wood to form a bow. Now, by twisting the twine around the straight stick, he could turn it by simply moving the bow back and forth. Another small piece of wood was needed to hold the top of the stick in place, but after a relatively short time, they were rewarded by a thin wisp of smoke rising from the bark. Very carefully, Eric added a tiny piece of moss and blew gently. A tiny, transparent yellow flame flickered up and died down. As his confidence grew, Eric added more moss and soon had a small fire going. The dry bark even caught and Eric added some twigs from the mat.

Feeling like Robinson Crusoe, Eric watched proudly as the fire grew. It didn't give off much heat, but the very fact that they had made it gave a tremendous feeling of satisfaction.

"See," said Rose gleefully, "I knew we could do it!"

"You were right," Eric admitted generously. This was a big enough achievement for them all to share.

"Fire, fire . . ." was all Weet could bring himself to say. He had been trying for three years to do this and Eric had done it in less than an hour. Surely he would be able to answer all his other questions too. But not tonight; already it was almost dark.

Exhausted by the day's events, the five unusual friends settled themselves on the mat facing the tiny, hopeful fire. A chorus of "good nights," echoed round before silence fell.

But Eric couldn't sleep. He was happy to be back and immensely proud of his fire-making prowess but, underneath it all, he was worried. He felt responsible for the others, but there was a loneliness that bothered him more. He had found the friend he had been yearning for for weeks, but did he have to lose his parents to do it? During his first visit to Weet's time, he had feared that a meteorite had destroyed his world and trapped him in Weet's. That had not happened, but this visit had a different beginning. His world had not been destroyed, but he could see no way that his parents, and probably himself, Rose and Sally, could have survived. That truck had been going flat out when it hit them. No one could have survived.

So was he dead? Would that mean he would stay here for eternity or would he flip back to his own time and be dead, whatever that might mean? And what about his parents? It was one thing to time travel and know that your parents were all right in the other world, but the thought that they were dead was too terrible, even if you could never know for sure. Tears filled Eric's eyes and spilled over onto the mat. He must never tell Rose how serious the accident had been. More responsibility!

When he had wished he could come back here, he

had imagined that it would be easy. In reality, however, it was very hard.

As he lay awake with the turmoil of his thoughts, the huge, alien moon rose to hover over the small group. It reminded Eric of another night when he had lain awake wondering how and why he could travel in time. Obviously, some mysterious link must exist between him and Weet. The first time they had met could have been chance, but not this time. What did it all mean? Eric was no closer to an answer when he eventually drifted off into an uneasy sleep.

# CHAPTER 9
## *the valley of death*

The night was bitterly cold. Not nearly as cold as the time Eric had gone camping with his Dad in the modern Rocky Mountains, but then he had been in a down sleeping bag. This time, he was only wearing light pants and a T-shirt, while Rose at least had a sweat shirt. Appropriately enough it was from the Royal Tyrrell Museum of Palaeontology with its impressive logo of a running Albertosaurus. The friends huddled together for warmth. Weet lay on the outside, farthest away from the tiny, glowing fire. Next to him lay Eric with his arm protectively draped over his sister. Rose, curled up around Sally, was the warmest of them all. Sinor, disdaining the messy huddle of bodies, perched slightly to one side with his head tucked protectively under his arm.

Even with all the shared warmth, it was an uncomfortable night. Eric had woken four or five times from a series of weird dreams. In one, he had been locked in a refrigerator. It was completely dark, but he knew he was there with Rose and his parents.

His Dad's voice in the darkness kept giving him practical but not very useful advice like "Jump up and down, it will help you keep warm." His mother kept saying things like "How many times must I tell you not to drink straight from the milk carton? Use a glass." Rose complained that she would die rather than eat yogurt, while Sally was chewing something in the meat compartment. Eric tried to call Weet for help, but all he could manage through his chattering teeth was an unintelligible mumble.

All at once a blinding light washed over the scene. Someone had opened the door. Eric wasn't scared, but he should have been. The figure standing in the doorway was a cross between Arnold Schwarzenegger and Tyrannosaurus rex. Trunk-like legs supported a grotesquely-muscled body which rippled beneath a dark green skin. On top sat the familiar head with its wide mouth, beady eyes and rows of sharp teeth.

"Yum," said the unlikely Arnold Rex, "lunch!" A long arm reached in and plucked Rose off the top shelf and lifted her towards the gaping jaws.

"Don't stand with the refrigerator door open," nagged Eric's Mom.

"Try punching it on the nose," added his Dad. "That works with sharks."

"Please don't dip me in yogurt," said the fast-disappearing Rose.

Eric screamed and leapt at the monster. "Don't eat my sister!" he shouted. But it was in vain. The farther Eric jumped, the farther away the monster seemed to be. With a horrible feeling that there was nothing he could do, Eric began to fall, down, down, down, until he landed, awake and cold, between Weet and Rose.

The sun was just beginning to show above the hilly horizon far to the east. Eric lay shivering for a short while, but soon the others were awake and movement seemed the only way to get warm. A branch in the fire still glowed and, in response to Eric's blowing, flared into a new blaze. As they warmed up and ate a breakfast of fruit, they began to look towards the day.

"I suppose we should move along the ridge," suggested Eric. "It's clear and seems to be taking us in the right direction."

Weet nodded in agreement and began putting the woven saddle back on the maiasaura. Eric and Rose foraged down the slope for fruit to fill the saddlebags. The fruit was scarce and tended to be small, but eventually they had enough to fill the bags and they returned to the waiting Weet.

For most of the morning the going was easy, if uncomfortable, and was certainly much faster than walking. The ridge was wide and clear of rocks and debris but, as they neared the still-smoking volcano, the ground became rougher and the going slower.

They were climbing quite steeply and the valleys on either side were flattening out until, when they drew level with the base of the volcano, they were crossing a broad plain.

The dust on the plain was only a few inches deep and didn't even trouble Sally and Sinor. What was potentially more trouble was the wide gully which opened in front of them. It appeared to be going in the right direction and began as little more than a shallow depression but, as they progressed, the sides became rugged and steep and Eric began to have the uncomfortable feeling of being trapped. The rocks around them were dark red and black, and smoke rose from cracks in the ground. The very earth itself felt insecure and they could feel a rumbling coming from beneath them as if some huge monster were snoring deep below. Small rocks were continually being dislodged from the surrounding walls and tumbled down with a scuttering noise. Keeping a straight course was hampered by the smoking patches of ground and the large rocks which littered the gully floor.

As they proceeded through the bleak landscape, Eric was relieved that every step was now taking them farther and farther from the belching volcano. Perhaps the worst was behind them.

It was not. The first sign of trouble was when one of the dislodged pebbles hit Eric a sharp blow on the shoulder. They were close to one of the valley walls, but there did seem to be more rocks falling about them now. In painful annoyance, Eric looked up. He was just in time to catch a fleeting glimpse of a figure disappearing behind a large rock halfway up the wall of the gorge.

"Weet," he shouted in alarm, "there's someone up there!"

Weet reined in their mount and followed Eric's extended arm. At first, there was nothing to be seen, but their halt encouraged the stone throwers and soon they could be seen darting out from cover and lobbing a rock at the friends before scurrying back. They seemed to be everywhere.

"Monkeys," said Rose in surprise.

"No," replied her brother, "they can't be monkeys. They must be some kind of dinosaur."

But they did look like monkeys. They were about as tall as Rose, and very slender in build. Their faces were long and pointed and had a permanently surprised expression, thanks to two bushy white eyebrows. The rest of the body was covered in dark brownish fur. What made Eric sure that he was not looking at monkeys was the short, hairless tail which was rigid and was held out behind for balance. The creatures were very agile and jumped around the rough walls with great ease.

Most of the stones were missing their mark,

but a few uncomfortably large ones were landing very close.

Eric was about to suggest that they move farther out to the centre when a particularly large rock hit Weet on the side of the head. Dropping the reins, he slid sideways and fell to the ground. Confused by the lack of control and the changing weight on its back, the maiasaura reared up on its hind legs. Eric grabbed at the reins, but it was too late. Awkwardly, he and his sister slid off the long back and landed in the rocky dust beside their friend. Frightened and stung by the sharp stones, the maiasaura crouched down defensively, before fleeing out into the gully.

Now there was no escape. Dismounted, they were easy targets and, gaining confidence all the time, the monkey-dinosaurs showered them with more and more stones. When Eric attempted to stand, an avalanche of stones forced him back to his knees. As the rocks rained down on their backs, Weet and Eric huddled over Rose, Sally and Sinor, awaiting the inevitable. Either they would be knocked unconscious or they would be buried in the ever growing mound of stones.

As Eric was fruitlessly pondering what he could do, he noticed that the volume of stones hitting his back seemed to be diminishing.

"They stop!" If Weet's whistling voice had been capable of inflection, he would have sounded

surprised. But he was right. The stones had stopped hitting their backs.

"If they've stopped, then get off me," came Rose's voice from the bottom of the protective pile. Driven by Rose's continued prompting, the friends gradually became disentangled. Eric ached all over and his back was covered in bruises. Weet had the cut on his head, but it had stopped bleeding. Rose, Sally and Sinor all seemed to be fine. As he stretched and scanned the gully walls, Eric spotted the last of their strange tormentors scuttling out of sight over the rim.

"They've gone," he said wonderingly. "We were at their mercy. Why did they stop stoning us?"

Before anyone had a chance to reply, Eric heard the train coming. At least, it sounded like a train. From a long way away beneath his feet, a train was speeding closer and closer. Eric remembered a story his grandmother had told him.

"Earthquake!" he yelled. "Get away from the wall!" Dragging his surprised sister, Eric struggled out to the centre of the valley. They were almost there, and the train had almost reached their station, when the ground lost control of itself. Suddenly, it dropped a foot only to shoot back up to painfully meet their falling bodies. Everyone was thrown flat by these wild gyrations.

"I'm going to be seasick," thought Eric dumbly as

he was tossed up and down. The rumbling train sound had became a deafening roar of tortured, crashing rock. Sections of the valley wall collapsed and cracks opened all over the floor. Out of them, jets of steam shot up to ten feet in the air. In other places, what looked like hot mud was bubbling to the surface to form miniature volcanoes. It was as if the earth had come alive and was trying to throw off or boil the annoying creatures which were crawling about on its surface.

After what seemed an eternity, but was really only a few seconds, the ground went back to doing what it should—nothing. The sudden stillness was overwhelming and no one said anything for some time. All was quiet apart from the occasional rattle of a loose stone finding a stable place to rest and the last hisses of the dying geysers. The air was hazy with dust.

"Wow!" was all Eric could say. Looking back to where they had been at the bottom of the gully wall, all he could see was a pile of rubble. If he had not remembered his grandmother saying that an earthquake she had been through in Africa had sounded just like a train, they would now be buried under it.

"Is everyone all right?" he asked eventually. A chorus of nods met his question.

"What happened?" a stunned Rose asked.

"An earthquake," replied her brother. "Probably just a local one caused by lava rising under the volcano. It might signal another eruption coming. We should get away. In any case, we don't want to wait for our hairy rock-throwing friends to return."

The maiasaura was sitting some thirty feet away with a dumber than usual look on its face. Fortunately, it too was so stunned by the experience that it offered no resistance to Weet's attempts to catch and remount it. Soon, shaken but not seriously hurt, the five friends were continuing on their way.

An hour or so after the earthquake, and much to Eric's relief, the gully widened into a grey plain which stretched off in a gradual slope in front of them. Now that they were safe from the rock-throwers, Eric, Rose and Weet dismounted. The plain was composed of grey, gravely rock in pieces ranging in size from a marble to a soccer ball. Eric bent down to examine the stones.

"Pumice," he said, picking up a large piece and holding it out to Rose. "See all the holes in it? Those are gas bubbles preserved from when this stuff was thrown out of the volcano."

"Great, now we're having a geology lesson." Rose was less than enthusiastic.

"Here, catch!" Eric playfully tossed the large rock he was holding at Rose. Startled, she jumped back, but instinctively tried to catch the flying object.

"Careful!" she said. "You could have hurt..." But her anger soon turned to wonder. "It's so light! It's not like a rock at all."

Eric laughed and tossed a piece to Weet. "It's the gas bubbles. The rock is riddled with them. They make it really light."

Soon the three had forgotten their aches and bruises and were playfully chucking lumps of rock at each other. Caught up in the general excitement, Sally and Sinor romped around at their feet.

"It feels like it's been a long day already," said Eric as soon as everyone had calmed down. He looked up at the sun. "But it's still only early afternoon. I suppose we should be making tracks. That looks like the right direction," he added, pointing down the pumice slope.

# CHAPTER 10

### the journey west

Eric remembered little of the next three days. They were all a blur of riding from dawn to dusk and shivering through long nights. It was tiring, but it was good to be with friends. The only problem was Eric's nagging worry about what had happened to his parents back in his own world. When he thought about it, he was swamped in waves of sadness at the thought that he and Rose might be orphans if they ever got back. He hid his sadness from Rose who gaily accepted the whole experience and only complained when she discovered bugs on the maiasaura's back.

They soon crossed the pumice desert and found themselves on a ridge running between two hills. Before them lay a broad plateau stretching ahead. It consisted of low rounded hills and wide valleys, which looked to Eric nothing like the magnificent, snow-covered mountains and echoing canyons they would later become. For that he was glad because it made their travelling much easier and they made good time.

The hilly plateau was high and supported few trees. Some were familiar pines, but the majority were a bushy type of deciduous tree with broad, three-pointed leaves, and none were more than 10 or 15 feet high. Between the trees, the ground was covered in low vegetation. Fortunately, much of the vegetation bore small berries which turned out to be quite tasty. Eric's favourites were the dark ones which reminded him of the sweet blueberries which had gone into his mother's delicious pies. There were also bitter ones rather like raspberries and small red ones which Eric guessed were related to huckleberries. It was not a varied diet, but it kept them going as they travelled along beneath the green-carpeted hills.

The weather was uniformly pleasant during the day. As time wore on, Eric and Rose both began to get the hang of moving comfortably with the maiasaura's rolling gait. The third day made Eric anxious because it marked the length of time they had been in Weet's world the previous visit. Mostly, however, the companions were too absorbed in physical activity to let their minds wander too far from their immediate surroundings.

Most of the wildlife was small: lizards and the occasional snake, which they avoided. Insects, both flying and crawling, were common but did not bother them too much. Surprisingly to Eric, birds also seemed to be quite common and advanced. Some were obviously flying reptiles, with long tails and teeth, but others, particularly some brightly-coloured, crow-sized creatures, were very bird-like. A variety of pteranodons swooped across the sky above the travellers, but none rivalled the size of the one the children had seen when they had first been introduced to Weet's world.

The land creatures consisted of dwarf, hairy versions of the hadrosaurs from the lowlands. These dinosaurs were only four or five feet tall when they reared up on their back legs. They had wide bills like the hadrosaurs and a range of colourful crests with a variety of odd shapes from straight spikes to broad antler-like growths. They seemed to feed on the berries and communicated through a complex range of whistles, snorts and grunts.

In addition to the hadrosaurs, there was a slender, graceful plant-eater, which reminded Eric in size and shape of an ostrich. Mostly, they balanced on their back legs and grazed the bushy trees. Their front legs were long and thin and were often used to hook branches and pull them down to mouth level. The head was small, narrow and balanced on a thin, sinuous neck. In front of enormously large eyes, it ended in a long beak with a brightly-coloured tip. The animals, with the exception of their tails and legs, were covered in coarse, yellowish hair. They moved about with a nervous, jerky motion and were so shy that, despite several attempts, Eric could never get close to them.

The reason for their shyness became obvious on the second day, when the companions stumbled upon a lunch scene. One of the tree-eaters was lying in a clearing by a stream. The obvious causes of its death were collected around the body, squabbling over who should have the tastiest bits. The diners were about the size of large cats and were covered in greenish-brown fur. Their heads were bare and bright blue in colour. Two  sharp, curved teeth protruded from the lower jaw upwards on each side of their squat snouts and were being used to cut up lunch in a remarkably efficient fashion.

The creatures preferred standing on all fours, but occasionally one would rear up and look around or sniff the air. When they noticed the group watching them, they stopped feeding and let out loud hissing noises, obviously designed to warn them away.

"OK, we don't want your lunch," said Eric hurriedly. "The berries are fine."

The group took a wide detour around the gruesome picnic. Eric doubted that he, Rose or Weet were in much danger from the beasts, but he kept a close eye on Sally and Sinor.

Towards evening each day they searched for a suitable clearing in which to camp. Clearings were fairly common, but it was nice to find one close to a stream where they could get a drink and wash off the dirt of the day. The bushes provided ample material for sleeping mats and for fires. Eric quickly became adept at fire lighting and even Weet managed one evening to get a respectable blaze going.

After the fire was built, the friends would sit on their mats and talk. Weet's mastery of English continued to progress by leaps and bounds until he was able to express complex ideas and understand most of what Eric said. On the other hand, attempts by Eric to learn Weet's whistling language were a dismal failure. When he tried, his mouth and tongue seemed far too rigid to mould themselves into the shapes necessary. He could produce the odd whistle, but stringing them together into words was an impossibility. Rose had better luck and, with Weet's delighted encouragement, even managed a few recognizable words. However, it was obvious that any meaningful communication would have to take place in Eric and Rose's language.

In these evening talks, Weet was anxious to find out all that Eric knew about his world. Eric was equally anxious not to tell Weet everything. It would hardly be polite to start talking about his favourite pastime—digging up dinosaur bones— when the owner of some of them was sitting across the fire from you.

The secrets Eric possessed about the extinction of the dinosaurs, combined with the secrets he kept to himself about the car crash that had brought them here, combined to weigh heavily on his mind. It seemed there was no escaping responsibility, in this world or his own.

Despite the restrictions on what Eric could say, he felt he had managed quite well to give Weet some sense of what his own world was like. But there were difficulties. It had been easy enough to say that the moon was smaller or the stars were different, but to try and get across a sense of what Calgary was like with its teeming people, high-rise buildings and noisy cars was next to impossible.

For Weet's part, he had managed to convey a good sense of what life was like in his world, mainly because his audience had experienced some of it and, in any case, it was all around them and he had lots of props to rely on. Eric was equally sure he could explain Calgary much better if they were in a Toyota driving down Centre Street.

Most interestingly, between them they had come up with a plausible explanation for the shovelbills' sickness. Weet's discovery that the beasts didn't feel cold before they died suggested that it was not the changing climate that was killing them, although the cold may have been making them more susceptible to sickness.

Eric considered the fact that there was no sickness where there were no velociraptors to be significant. This, combined with Weet's stories of the sickleclaws appearing from the north lands, seemed to support a theory that he had read about diseases being brought across the land bridge between North America and Asia.

Unwittingly, Weet supplied another piece of the puzzle. On the second night they had been lying awake when the clear sky was suddenly enlivened by a burst of shooting stars. It was simply a small patch of cosmic dust encountered on Earth's long, lonely voyage around the galaxy, but it reminded Weet of the fire nights. These occurred every year at about the same time.

Weet remembered the previous year. On that night there had also been a display of shooting stars, but these had been much bigger. They had lit up the sky as bright as day and driven the entire family out of their tree ring to watch. The lines of fire appeared in the east, over the sea, and sped across the sky to disappear behind the mountains. It had been nothing but a spectacular display, but Weet's father remembered a time when several had landed nearby and caused considerable damage. He also remembered a time when there had been no such thing as the fire nights. That had been a time before the nights began getting cold.

Eric listened in silence, but in his mind he was wondering. Was this a sign of the coming end? Obviously, every year, the Earth passed through a cloud of cosmic debris, some of which was large enough to reach the ground and do damage before burning up. Did there lurk, in the centre of this cloud, a rock ten kilometres across which, one year, was destined not to miss Weet's world? It took Eric a long time to fall asleep that night.

# CHAPTER 11

## *losing a friend*

**B**y the fourth day of travelling, the trees had increased both in size and number. There were still open areas, but picking a direct route was becoming progressively harder. About noon, they crested the top of a ridge and saw a sight that took their breath away. The land fell away to a lush, green plain which ended in a broad, white, sandy beach. The distant blue could only be the Pacific Ocean. A large river poured through a gorge in the hills to their right and cut a meandering path across the sand plain to the head of a broad inlet. On the horizon, dark, misty lumps indicated the presence of a large offshore island.

The three companions dismounted and stood in silence for several minutes until Weet uttered one whistling word.

"Home."

To Eric and Rose it didn't feel much like home, but it was undoubtedly impressive.

"It's so beautiful!" Rose was obviously

overwhelmed by the sight. "That's the biggest beach I've ever seen."

"Yeah," Eric agreed, "with the moon being closer, the tidal range will be huge."

Eric was also amazed that the pleasant hills over which they had been walking would, one day, be uplifted and scarred to become the Coast Mountains.

"I wonder if that's Vancouver Island in the distance?" he mused out loud. "It's pretty big, but then I have no idea where we are. That island could completely disappear by the time Gran comes to live here."

It was all wild guesswork. All the maps Eric had seen of Western Canada in the Late Cretaceous had either stopped at the Alberta border or had shown the coast in dotted lines interspersed with question marks. A lot could happen in 65 million years.

What bothered him more was that the land below lacked the open clearings found on the other side of the mountains. The trees formed a continuous canopy over the ground. Eric had visions of the South American jungle, with its impenetrable masses of creepers and underbrush. Despite the warm air, Eric shivered at the thought of struggling through jungle inhabited by the predators Weet had described—predators that had driven Weet's people away from their land. But there was no point in mentioning his fears now. They had no choice but to descend into the thick greenery before them.

"Barbecued hot dogs on the beach tonight!" joked Eric, setting off down the slope. "Last one in the water buys the cokes."

Leading the maiasaura by the reins, it didn't take the party long to descend into the trees and, to Eric's great relief, travelling through them was relatively easy. Most of the trees were huge and smooth-trunked, rather like the familiar cedars from before. Interspersed were coarser-barked firs and occasional clumps of deciduous trees. Regardless of type, every tree trunk was huge, making Eric feel very small. The branches didn't begin till well above Eric's head, but they soon formed an impenetrable canopy that almost blotted out the sunlight and made the whole scene dark. The soft and spongy ground between the trees was covered with a mat of pine needles and cones. The only low vegetation were ferns, which seemed to thrive where the ground was boggy, and a few low bushes with broad dark green leaves.

The company moved on in awed silence. Oddly enough, despite the gloom and intimidating size of his surroundings, Eric felt strangely comfortable and relaxed here. At one point, he thought he spotted some movement in the branches and had the distinct sense of being watched, but it soon passed and he put it down to tricks of the forest light. Weet was obviously delighted to be in the land of his ancestors. He continuously examined his surroundings with great interest.

After about three hours, the group emerged from the forest. The brilliant light of the late afternoon sun illuminated a vast expanse of blindingly white sand. From the hilltop, it had looked flat and featureless, but close-up it reminded Eric of pictures he had seen of the Sahara desert. Small sand dunes marched across the plain in orderly rows. None was more than eight or ten feet high, but they were undoubtedly sand dunes. In the hollows between them and on some of the gentler slopes, sword-like grass and small, rugged-looking shrubs were clinging to life.

"Wow," Rose said, awe-struck. "That's the biggest beach I've ever seen."

"I don't think it's a beach," said Eric thoughtfully.

"Of course it is!" Rose knew sand when she saw it. "We saw the ocean from the hill."

"Yes," Eric agreed, "but I don't think the tide ever comes this far. Those plants couldn't survive if it did and the sand dunes look like they have been formed by the wind, not the ocean. Maybe it was a beach at one time."

Rose was only half listening, but Weet wasn't listening at all. He had turned and was looking back the way they had come. This was not because he didn't find the beach impressive, but something more incredible was demanding his attention. Rose gasped as she followed his gaze. About fifteen feet away, standing in the shadow of the trees, was another Weet. This one was smaller, more lightly built and considerably paler in colour, but it was undoubtedly very closely related to their friend. Around its neck hung a necklace of tiny, intricately coiled shells which glinted in the sun with iridescent blues, reds and purples.

"Eric!" Rose's voice was soft but urgent.

Oblivious to all but the sandy view before him, Eric continued his speculations. "If I remember correctly, the sea level was falling at the end of the Cretaceous ..."

"ERIC!" This time there was no mistaking the urgency. Eric looked around and gasped even louder than his sister.

The newcomer eyed them all closely, before breaking into a string of whistling sounds remarkably like Weet's. Instinctively, Eric and Rose glanced over at Weet to see if he understood. Their friend remained motionless and gave no indication that he had even heard.

But Weet's brain was in turmoil. There were survivors! Here was one of his ancestors who had stayed behind in paradise and not chosen exile on the other side of the world. Someone who represented a continuity with the past and a hope for the future. Someone who could answer some of his questions and help him understand the world of his past and, perhaps, the future. The creature before him had been separated from his people for generations, yet it looked like him, spoke his language and, most vivid in Weet's mind at the moment, she was the most beautiful thing he had ever seen.

"Who are you?" she asked in a voice that was light and airy, yet strangely foreign. He could understand her, so she would understand him.

"I am Weet," he replied formally. "These are Eric, Rose, Sa"y and Sinor," he continued, indicating the rest of the small group. "We are from over there." He gestured back through the trees.

Now it was the stranger's turn to regard them in silence.

"That way is Fire Mountain. No one lives there," she said eventually. Before Weet could explain further, she shook her head as if suddenly remembering something, looked quickly around and continued, "I am Saar, but we must go before the sickleclaws find us. Come."

Eric had not understood any of the conversation, but it was obvious that this stranger wanted them to follow. Where to, he had no idea, but Weet seemed comfortable and beckoned for them to come.

"Where are we going?" asked Rose suspiciously as they set off.

"I don't know," her brother replied, "but, wherever it is, we seem to be in a hurry." Grabbing the maiasaura's reins, he followed their new guide back into the trees.

The group moved at a rapid pace roughly parallel to the beach. Eric guessed they were heading for the large river they had seen from the ridge. Their guide was extremely agile, dancing around tree trunks and over exposed roots and stopping frequently to urge the others on. Eric had to concentrate to find the best route for the beast he was leading and he struggled to keep up.

As they progressed, the trees became steadily smaller until Weet had to duck to avoid the occasional branch. The maiasaura was having less luck. Eric was running out of breath and was about to ask Weet for a rest break, when he spotted a movement in the shadows off to his right. He glanced over, but all he could see were the mottled patches of dark and light where the sun filtered through the trees. Another movement caught the corner of his eye behind him. Instinctively, he glanced over his shoulder. At that moment, his feet decided to have an argument with an exposed tree root. His feet lost. With a surprised shout, Eric tumbled forward onto the soft carpet of pine needles.

Almost immediately, strong hands grabbed his shoulders and unceremoniously hoisted him to his feet. The new member of the group was whistling urgently and pointing into the shadows. As Eric looked, the mottled shadows slowly resolved themselves into shapes and his heart sank.

"Velociraptors!" he gasped. He recognized them despite the obvious differences from the ones he had encountered before. These ones were smaller, not being much taller than Eric's waist. They were covered in feathers, but not the yellow and black ones Eric was familiar with. These feathers were a patchwork of muddy brown and paler green which allowed them to blend in perfectly with the dappled sunlight beneath the trees. Despite the differences from their cousins across the mountains, Eric was certain that the rows of teeth and the deadly claws on the hind feet would function much the same once they got within range.

As Eric's eyes became accustomed to the creatures' camouflage, the full horror of their situation began to dawn on him. There were at least twenty of the beasts, warily circling the small group at the limit of vision. They were silent, but every so often, one would raise a crest of feathers on the back of its head to display a bright flash of colour. Mostly they held their bodies horizontally, which made them look smaller, but no less threatening. Occasionally, one would lift its head and silently bare its teeth. The motion was accompanied by a raising of the rigid tail until it formed a V with the body. Some accompanied this movement with an impressive hop which, Eric was dismayed to see, often carried the creature higher than his own head. He was not thrilled at the prospect of meeting those dagger-like claws at eye level.

Their guide whistled urgently, not in an attempt to disable the velociraptors, but to communicate with Weet. Suddenly, she broke into a run.

"Come!" Weet shouted and pushed Rose and Eric after her.

Eric could see no point in running, but he followed as fast as he could. Oddly, their new companion was running through the trees with her arms held high as if in surrender. Eric didn't think the velociraptors took prisoners. Weet was running beside Rose. Out of the corners of his eyes, Eric could see the velociraptor pack moving beside them. They were fast and had already pulled ahead and would soon cut off their retreat. After that, it would all be over pretty quickly.

Eric glanced over his shoulder at the maiasaura. It was gasping and obviously confused and in some distress. Its eyes were open wide and flicked nervously from one side to the other. The closest velociraptor was only about five feet away now.

Eric looked ahead. Their guide was gone! He barely had time to register this fact before his world

turned upside down. He saw a flash of green, felt
something grip him under the shoulders and,
incredibly, his feet were running in mid-air. The
maiasaura's rein was pulled sharply and painfully
through his hand. His momentum carried him up in
an arc until he was among the tree branches. One
large branch was just about to make painful contact
with his stomach when a pair of hands appeared
from nowhere, grasping his waist and firmly setting
him on the wide flat area where branch joined trunk.
Almost instantly, Rose was deposited at his side.

Eric looked down just in time to see a figure
wrapped around the branch below reach down, grasp
Weet's upstretched arms and haul him up into the
tree. As soon as he was up, Weet whistled, Sinor
jumped and was deftly caught by another pair of
arms. Confused by this vanishing act, the
velociraptors concentrated on their remaining
chance at a meal. Sally and the maiasaura were the
only ones left on the ground. Barking furiously, Sally
was circling the tree into which her friends had so
mysteriously vanished. Not being as tall as Eric or as
agile as Sinor, the rescuing hands couldn't reach her.

"Sally!" Eric's desperate cry only made the poor
dog rush about in greater panic. The velociraptors
seemed to be having trouble deciding how to handle
this small, rapidly moving prey. As Eric watched in
horror, several lunging attacks only just missed his

pet. Inevitably, one of the attackers made contact. It was only a swipe with the side of the foot, but it bowled Sally over. As she lay winded, the velociraptors closed in.

At the last possible moment, a green flash arced down and lifted the dog high above her attackers' heads. Like acrobats at the circus, one of their rescuers had wrapped his knees around the lowest branch while holding the ankles of a companion. This acrobatic manoeuvre enabled the lower of the two to grab Sally and deposit her in Eric's arms.

That only left the maiasaura. The poor beast was stumbling around in panic below them. It was now the sole focus for the hungry velociraptor pack.

"Can't we help it?" Rose asked, near tears. Weet looked over at Saar and shook his head. There was no way they could get a full grown hadrosaur up into the trees. Eric felt tears welling up in his eyes, for he had grown fond of the lumbering beast during their journey.

The velociraptors were very close to the maiasaura now. As if sensing that it had no hope, the object of their attention had stopped stumbling around and stood completely still, watching its attackers.

Even though he was expecting it, the attack surprised Eric with its swiftness. As if in response to an unseen command, the velociraptors pounced.

Unlike the ones Eric knew, they leapt in unison and the maiasaura was suddenly transformed into a quivering, feathery mass. The maiasaura threw its head back and let out a single, hoarse scream. Carrying its deadly burden, it stumbled into the nearest tree, fell to the ground, and lay still. The kill was quick and efficient, leaving the creatures to feed at their leisure.

As Eric gazed down in wonder and horror, one of the velociraptors left the dead maiasaura and came over to the tree in which Eric was hiding. It stood at the bottom and looked up. Then it sprang. Eric drew back in fear, but he was high enough that the beast couldn't reach him. Instead of falling back, the velociraptor dug its blood-flecked claws into the trunk and hung on about three feet below Eric. It made no attempt to climb higher, but simply hung there, eyeing him. Eric felt certain that there was a rational purpose behind the creature's actions and he felt sure he recognized some level of intelligence in the eyes, which stared coldly at him from the narrow skull.

Eventually, with a last defiant flaring of its brightly feathered crest, the velociraptor dropped back to resume its meal. Rose was sobbing quietly and everyone else was standing in silence. Saar whistled softly and the group organized itself and moved off through the trees.

# CHAPTER 12

## the ancestor's story

Eric enjoyed climbing trees. Even a broken wrist three years ago when he had miscalculated the strength of a branch in the local park had not dampened his enthusiasm. But he had never been in trees like these. The branches were as wide as his body and, where they joined the imposing trunk, they splayed out to form a wide, vaguely saucer-shaped platform. Each branch was bare for a considerable distance away from the trunk, creating the effect of being in an old building which had been propped up by the haphazard placement of supporting beams. The branches were far enough apart to allow Eric and his strange rescuers to walk upright. Weet, however, had a problem. He was easily the tallest creature around and had to assume a semi-crouching posture.

After they had travelled far enough to be out of sight and earshot of the feasting velociraptors, Saar waved the group to a halt and Eric had a chance to examine their rescuers.

Five of these new creatures were now part of their group. All were noticeably shorter than Weet and much lighter in colour. They also had a lighter frame and looked quite at home balanced casually on the surrounding branches.

After the escape, Weet seemed unusually subdued. He gazed fixedly at one of the strangers in particular. From the shell necklace, Eric recognized her as the first one they had met. No one seemed in a hurry to make the first move. As usual, it was Rose who broke the silence. Leaning sideways, she touched Weet on the hip.

"Who are they?" she asked.

The touch startled Weet out of his reverie. He looked down at Rose, then across at Eric. Indicating the stranger in front of them, he said: "Saar, she my. . ." he hesitated, searching for the right word. "Mother, mother, mother, mother, mother," he concluded a little lamely.

Eric was confused. This couldn't be Weet's mother.

"What do you mean?" Rose asked.

Weet repeated his odd statement.

Suddenly, it dawned on Eric what his friend meant. "The ancestors," he said slowly. "These are Weet's ancestors who never left the coast, or at least their descendants. They did take to the trees and they did survive." Weet nodded encouragement as Eric continued, "It would be like us going back to

Scotland where Dad's folks came from 150 years ago and finding a branch of our family. Except they left because the crops failed, not because they were being chased by dinosaurs."

The five ancestors looked on with blank stares. One of them surreptitiously rubbed its nose. Saar turned to Weet.

"What are they?" she asked, indicating Eric and Rose. "Where are they from? Why do they have a large marat with them? They certainly are ugly."

Weet had become accustomed to his friends' appearance, but he could remember the revulsion he had felt when he first saw them.

"They are humans . . ." Weet tried to remember Eric's explanations. "They smell strange and they seem stupid, but they can perform wonders. They can make fire. The marat is their pet, like Sinor." Weet was rambling a bit, partly because of the difficulty of explaining Eric, Rose and Sally to a stranger, and partly because of Saar herself. Whenever he looked at her, he felt confused and silly. "They are from," Weet hesitated, "another place. A place far away where many people live in boxes made from bits of trees and ride about in animals called cars." This was getting ridiculous. Weet was talking nonsense. "They are my friends," he concluded lamely.

Saar had listened to all this in silence. Now she continued to fix Weet with a gaze that made him feel as if he were about to pass out. Then she nodded, as if satisfied.

"We must go now and discuss this with the Trium. Come."

Before Eric could react, one of the ancestors picked up Sally and the group moved off along the branch.

"What's going on?" Eric asked Weet.

Weet was still gazing numbly at Saar. Eric nudged his friend and repeated the question.

Weet turned as if awakening from a dream. "We must go," was all he could manage before he followed her off into the foliage.

"It doesn't seem like we have much choice," Eric said to his sister. "Come on, let's go and see what happens next."

The journey through the trees was relatively easy. Close to the trunks, the branches were wide enough to walk on comfortably. Farther out, where they narrowed, the ancestors helped Eric and Rose along. At their ends, the branches were often intertwined with those of the next tree. In some cases, this intertwining was deliberate, with branches tied together by thick creepers.

After a while Eric began to get the impression that they were following a definite route. Sometimes they had to change levels to a branch above or below them. At these points, creepers were conveniently dangling and, in one case, a short ladder had been constructed. The group travelled in silence, concentrating on their footing. Out of the corners of his eyes, Eric occasionally saw movement on the ground below and, more frequently as they progressed, amongst the branches around them.

Eventually, the group reached an area which resembled a sort of market. Branches had been cut away and platforms had been built on the remaining ones to provide solid footing. These were on different levels, but connected by ladders. The overall effect was that of some kind of weird mall without escalators and clothes stores. In place of the clothes stores, each platform had a number of ramshackle stalls. Most of these carried displays of what Eric assumed were fresh fruits and vegetables. A few were familiar from Weet's country or from their travels, but many he had never seen before.

Some stalls reminded Eric of the old-fashioned Chinese shops he had seen in Vancouver. Rows of brown, dried things hung from racks and defied identification. Unlike Weet's people, the ancestors didn't appear to be strict vegetarians. Some stalls had a variety of dried fish and others displayed what appeared to be small birds, hung by their feet. Underneath was an assortment of eggs. Eric wondered whether, given the fact that all dinosaurs laid eggs, all the ones on display here belonged to birds.

As usual, Rose provided an ongoing chorus of grunts and yecchs as she spotted the more disgusting-looking displays. Despite his rumbling stomach, Eric had to admit that the look of the food did little for his appetite. The only stall that appeared to meet with Rose's approval didn't sell food at all, but shells. Piles of all kinds, from the rainbow shades of curved, iridescent ammonites to more common clam shells, were scattered around on woven mats. Behind the mat sat an obviously ancient, wrinkled ancestor. His body was almost entirely covered in strings of various shells. Eric was sure he would rattle if he were to get up and walk.

As they moved through the market, they were regarded with curiosity by the stall owners. Adults fell silent as they passed and burst into whispered, whistling conversation behind them. Children, always less inhibited, scurried around them, pointing and whistling gleefully.

Soon they had gathered quite a following of curious onlookers. Most swung down from the upper branches to the market levels with surprising agility. All wore shell jewellery of some sort, but none was as beautiful as Saar's necklace or as overdone as the collection worn by the old stall owner.

Eventually, the group reached a platform cleverly built around the trunks of several particularly large trees. There were no stalls here and Eric guessed that it was some kind of communal meeting place. Across the open space the trees ended and the platform became a balcony extending over the incredibly blue waters of a sizable river. Rope ladders descended to the water's edge where a collection of small boats made of bark and resembling fat, blunt canoes, was tied. Near the banks, the shallow river flowed slowly, but towards the middle the sandy bottom disappeared beneath the dark, swirling water.

The curious onlookers gathered around the edges of the platform or perched on branches. Sally, set down gently on her own four paws, scuttled over to huddle at Eric's feet. Even Sinor seemed subdued by the strange events of the previous half-hour and stayed close to Weet.

"I hope this is where they welcome new and honoured guests," Eric said, expressing their common anxiety. Just because these creatures looked like Weet, and might even be his distant relatives, did not mean that they would be as hospitable as Weet had been. After all, the homs had been less than friendly and this culture had obviously developed a lifestyle all its own. Eric looked around at the circle of faces. They didn't look aggressive, but it was hard to tell what was going on behind those expressionless masks. A noise overhead turned everyone's attention to a large group descending slowly through the branches.

With some shuffling about, the new arrivals arranged themselves in order of importance. The three figures at the front were obviously old and very important. Each wore circles of brightly coloured shells around its head, arms and legs. The one in the middle stepped forward, cupped its hands and bowed slightly in greeting. Eric took this as an encouraging sign. Then it spoke. Eric and Rose looked at Weet.

Weet's mind and heart were in turmoil. His mind had trouble accepting the impossible, these survivors of his people who had taken to living in the trees. His heart stirred at the sight of Saar gazing at him from behind the three old ones. With a start, he realized that the old one in the centre was addressing him.

"We welcome you here to our land. I am Seel, these are Saura and Sam," he said, indicating the old ones on either side of him. "We are the Trium. It is our job to welcome you and find out if what Saar tells us is true. She tells us you came from Fire Mountain?"

Weet felt the pressure of dozens of pairs of eyes fixed on him, waiting for his reply. Even Eric and Rose were staring at him. Slowly he stepped forward with cupped hands and bowed. A soft murmur swept through the crowd.

"We are happy to be here amongst you," he began politely. "I am Weet." At this, the murmur grew louder. Weet hesitated but continued, "This is Eric and this is Rose, and these are Sa"y and Sinor. We do not come from Fire Mountain, but from beyond." Another, louder gasp escaped the assembled multitude. Again, Weet hurried on.

"We passed near to Fire Mountain and it tried to trap us, but we escaped and journeyed to you."

"There is nothing across the mountain," the elder called Sam interrupted. "It is the edge of the world. You lie."

"No!" Weet hadn't meant it to come out quite so harshly, but he wasn't prepared to let this old man, ancestor or not, deny what he knew to be true. He could feel the tension in the crowd. Every head stretched forward as if fearful of missing a single word. Sam looked like he was about to explode.

"You dare to contradict me?" he breathed dangerously through his anger. "I will feed you and your ugly friends to the sickleclaws before I will listen to more lies." To the other members of the Trium, he added, "We have seen the warnings in the sky and here is the proof. They are lying, even using the name of Weet to trick us. We must not listen to them."

"Calm yourself brother," Seel interrupted. "These strange creatures have obviously been turned mad by the horrors they experienced at the edge of the world."

Turning to Weet, he continued, "Once, long ago,

there was a time when no sickleclaws lived here. The people lived on the ground and the great water lapped at the roots of the trees. It was a time of peace and plenty when all we could wish for was here for the taking. But the sickleclaws came from the cold northlands and the people had no protection against them."

Weet listened in wonder as he realized that he was hearing his father's story.

"The sickleclaws were clever," continued Seel. "They hunted us for food, but also for sport and to teach their young how it was done. Some of the people took to hiding in the trees to escape, but each year they had to come down for the hatching.

"One year the sickleclaws attacked the hatching. They attacked in hundreds and killed a great many of the people. Some of the tree dwellers fled to the forest to hide in the trees, while others set out to escape across the mountains.

"Those in the trees were few and fearful. They had rescued no young from the hatching and could see no way to survive. Many began saying that they, too, should try to cross the mountains.

"One day, a stranger arrived. He was the only survivor of the group that went to the mountains. He was exhausted and strangely silent, but when he heard that some wanted to try to cross the mountains, he told his story.

"When the hatching had been attacked, the stranger had persuaded a group to head for the mountains. At first, the going had been easy and the food was plentiful. It seemed as if they had made the right decision. On the third day their journey became more difficult. Ahead lay a mountain which smoked and belched fire. Even the very ground beneath their feet roared and moved as if in pain. The stranger was afraid and hung back. The companions he had encouraged pressed on. As they crossed a distant ridge, the mountain burst into flames. Black smoke poured out and fire shot into the sky. It was so hot even the rocks burned as they flew through the air. The earth shook and cracked and the group on the ridge disappeared. A choking, hot wind blew from the mountain and forced the stranger back the way he had come. He never saw his friends, or his mate, again.

"Somehow he retraced his steps to the people in the trees. He said Fire Mountain marked the edge of the world and warned us never to go that way or we would surely die. With no hope of escape, the people decided to stay. In time, the stranger became a great leader and laid the foundations for our way of life in the trees. He saved us all. He told us the truth about the mountains and gave us the strength to stay and build a future here. So you see," Seel finished his story almost sadly, "you cannot be telling the truth. There is nothing beyond Fire Mountain."

Weet stood in silence. His dreams were in ruins. His quest worthless. All the ancestors could offer him was their version of his father's story. And all they could do was live their lives the way they always had. It was a life different from the one he had left behind, but it was not a life that held any answers for the future.

There was only one question that Weet still wanted answered.

"What was the stranger's name?"

Seel regarded his tall visitor silently for a moment before whispering, "The stranger's name was Weet."

# CHAPTER 13

*prisoners again*

**E**ric had watched Weet's exchange with Seel with curiosity. Judging by the crowd's reactions, something important was happening, but he had no idea what. It was like being back in the hom village where they had been held prisoner during their first trip to Weet's time. But at least now there was the hope that Weet would be able to explain what was going on later. Everyone's attention was completely focused on the figures of Weet and Seel deep in conversation. Only Rose broke the silence, whispering annoyingly "What's happening?" as if Eric had suddenly become fluent in Weet's language and was deliberately not telling her what was going on. Even Sinor sat beside them with his head cocked in apparent interest. Sally, with pointed unconcern, lay asleep at Rose's side.

During the course of the meeting, the sun had set and the gathering had been slowly plunged into the silvery gloom of the moon. It was full and cast an ethereal glow over everything, giving the impression that this was a meeting of ghosts. Beyond the balcony, the river glittered like a stream of diamonds.

Finally, after a few last words of instruction, the three ancient ancestors and their retinue retreated back up into the trees. Amidst a chorus of muttered discussions, the crowd broke up. Two ancestors stepped forward and, after a short conversation with Weet, led the friends off the platform and through the trees parallel to the river. In the semi-dark, the going was slow, but they did not go far and were soon ushered onto a small platform next to a very substantial trunk. At the back of the platform was an area carpeted by leaves and covered by a canopy of woven creepers and branches. The side facing the platform was open. The other side of the platform overlooked a thirty-foot drop to the river.

"This must be our room for the night," quipped Eric, "No need to pick up a key from the front desk. I hope no one walks in their sleep."

No sooner had their guides left than two others appeared with trays of fruit and dried fish.

"Ah, room service," said Eric, continuing his lame joke, but no one laughed.

In weary silence, the group nibbled the most appealing portions of their rather odd supper. Eric and Sally both tried some of the dried fish and Eric pronounced it not too bad, but everyone else stayed with the recognizable fruit. After they had been eating for a few minutes and the worst of the hunger had abated, Eric could contain himself no longer.

"What happened, Weet?" he asked his friend. "Are they your ancestors? Are they glad to see you? Are they friendly?"

Weet took a long time to answer.

"Ancestors," he began slowly, "they not know answers. They think I lie."

Haltingly and with many breaks to search for an explanation, the story of what had happened came out. Weet's disappointment at not finding solutions to the problems of his world cast a cloak of sadness over everything he said. To Eric, it seemed that the only time he perked up was when he was talking about Saar.

Once the whole story was told, Eric wasn't sure why Weet was so despondent. Certainly no significant answers had been provided, but apart from the one old man threatening to feed them to the velociraptors, Eric felt things had gone quite well. They were safe for the moment and at least they were being fed.

However, if he were honest with himself, Eric had to admit to a feeling of guilt deep down below the warm, well-fed glow in his stomach. Weet wanted answers and had braved death to come here and get them. He was crushed now that he saw that the ancestors could not help him, but only had a collection of myths much like his own. They were just as tied to their ways as Weet's family was on the other side of the mountain. Eric wondered in passing whether he would have been similarly disappointed had he made it to Vancouver and confided his secrets to his Gran. He would never know now. But what he did know, he was reluctant to share. Eric knew what would happen to Weet's world and perhaps, unpleasant though it was, Weet would have been glad of that answer, rather than none at all.

Why was Eric burdened with so many secrets? All he had wanted was to return to Weet's world, learn more about it, and see his friend again. He hadn't asked for the knowledge he had or for the responsibility of having to keep it a secret. And secrets made him think of his parents. If he and Rose were stuck here forever, he would have to tell her about the crash eventually. But not tonight. He was tired and his memories of the maiasaura's end made him sad.

Worn out by their adventures, the small party finally curled up and drifted off into sleep.

Eric woke to the first rays of sunlight pushing through the foliage. He had slept better than he had expected and felt refreshed. Around him the others were stirring. Weet was at the opening of their shelter where someone had left a tray of fruit.

"Breakfast," said Eric airily. "These ancestors seem very considerate. I hope they're not fattening us up for the pot." Immediately he regretted the joke.

"They wouldn't do that, would they?" asked Rose, horrified.

"No, no," Eric added quickly, "it was just a joke."

"Well, I don't think it's funny," said his sister, turning away and tucking into a piece of nan. "I think these people are nice and we're lucky to be here. Would you rather be down on the ground with the veloci-things?"

Eric had to admit that he wouldn't. He attempted to lighten the mood a bit.

"Well, ladies and gentlemen, we have a morning at leisure in Ancestorville. You may want to rest in the hotel or take a short tour of the market. Perhaps a canoe trip on the Mososaur River to the fabled Ammonite Beach, where you can write your name in the sand to confound scientists millions of years in the future. It is your choice."

Rose smiled at Eric's imitation of a tour guide.

"I'd like to collect shells for a necklace like the lovely one that Saar wears," she added brightly.

"And you shall!" said Eric with mock drama. "We

will deck you out in so many shells that you'll put that old guy at the market to shame."

The children laughed. Weet liked to hear that odd, gurgling sound but, even if it had been possible, he didn't feel like joining in. He was still disappointed and yearned for Saar but, in the back of his mind, there was an uncomfortable feeling lurking. They were obviously a threat to the ancestors or at least were seen as one by some. If some of the ancestors believed the stories of the world beyond Fire Mountain, then Weet and his friends were undermining the foundations of their society. Some might attempt to escape life in the trees and the sickleclaws, and that would lessen the power of the leaders. Seel and his companions would not be too happy about that possibility.

After breakfast, the friends decided to take a look around the tree city. That was when they got the first sense that all was not well. Outside the shelter stood two ancestors. They wore no shell jewellery, but carried dangerous-looking clubs. Each club was close to three feet long and ended in a large knot of wood. They reminded Eric of the Zulu war-club his gran had on her wall in Vancouver. He had been allowed to play with that on one occasion and had some sense of the damage it could inflict on flesh and bone.

The two new ancestors did not threaten the group, but they stood blocking their way out and refused to move. They also ignored Weet's questions and Eric had the impression they would stop at nothing to prevent their guests from leaving.

"Why won't they let us leave?" demanded Rose.

"Probably they don't want us going down and scaring the velociraptors," joked Eric. "I imagine it's for our own protection. Why else would they keep us prisoner here?"

Rose appeared to accept this, but Eric certainly could think of a very good reason for keeping them prisoner: their knowledge of the world past Fire Mountain.

The morning passed slowly and mostly in silence as the three friends wrestled with their own thoughts. Around noon, more fruit was delivered.

"At least, they're not trying to starve us," Eric observed.

The meal was interrupted by a rustling at the back of their shelter. All three turned to see Saar poking her head through a hole in the branches. She whispered some urgent words at Weet who immediately turned back and said, "Keep eat. Look out."

Anxiously, Eric and Rose obeyed while Weet carried out a furtive conversation with Saar. Eventually the soft whistling stopped and Weet rejoined them to sit in silence. Finally, with an almost human shrug, he turned to Eric and said, "There is danger."

Eric's heart sank. He had almost convinced himself that the guards really were for their own protection.

"What danger?" Rose asked, so loudly that Weet signalled her to keep quiet.

"Saar say Trium feed we sickleclaw." The words were halting, but the message was crystal clear.

"What?" exclaimed Rose, forgetting the earlier injunction to be quiet. "They can't do that. Why would they want to do that?"

"Because," explained Eric, "they don't want the people to know that there is a world beyond Fire Mountain. The story that the original Weet brought back is the main thing that keeps everyone living this life in the trees, continually threatened by the velociraptors."

"But they seem to enjoy life here," Rose interrupted.

"Yes," continued Eric, "but there are other problems too. I'll bet the sea level is falling and they have to go farther and farther to get their food. That makes it even more dangerous."

Weet was watching Eric with concentration and nodded often. "Also others gone," he added.

"What?" asked Eric.

"Some left, gone islands," Weet explained.

"You mean, some of the city people have left and gone to live on some islands?" said Eric.

Weet nodded again.

"Outcasts," said Eric wonderingly. "People who don't like being ruled by the Trium and are attempting to find another way. I'll bet that's it. And the Trium is terrified that what we know will encourage more people to join them. Terrified enough to kill us to stop our story being believed."

"Tell them that we won't say anything!" Rose sounded very worried. "We'll go away and never come back."

"They can't risk it," said Eric. Then another thought struck him. "Especially with Weet's name. Their great hero who saved them originally was called Weet. If another Weet comes along and begins telling them something else, who knows what might happen."

"What are we going to do?" Both children looked at Weet.

Weet had no answer for them. He was as surprised at the violent reaction of the Trium as they were. He had hoped for some help with his questions. He knew it had been a slim hope, but he had not thought he would have to die for it. And there was something else he hadn't told his friends.

"I go," he added.

"What?" Eric was beginning to panic now too. "Where? Why?"

Weet didn't know all the answers himself. He only

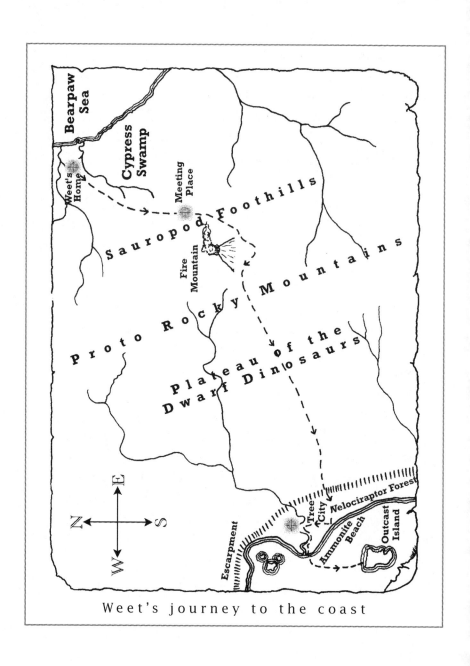

Weet's journey to the coast

knew that Saar had said it was imperative that he go with her to arrange for an escape that night. One of the group had to learn the route and Weet was the only one who could move through the city without arousing too much suspicion.

"I back," he attempted to explain. "Night, go island."

With a last look at his friends, he slipped quietly to the back of the shelter and out the hole to join Saar. Sinor appeared unsure and looked from Eric to Rose to Sally. Eventually, he decided to stay. Rose was close to panic.

"What's happening!" she wailed, loud enough that the two guards glanced over.

"Shh," said Eric. "Weet will come back for us. I think the plan is to escape tonight to the islands where the outcasts live. We have to stay here and hide the fact that Weet is missing."

Rose calmed a little. "OK," she said slowly, "but I hope Weet isn't too long, I get awfully lonely without him."

Eric felt the same way too, and silently wished that they were back in Weet's home circle with only the tyrannosaurus to worry about. The two children settled down in the mouth of the shelter, attempted to cover as much of the dark depths as possible, and waited to see what would happen next.

# CHAPTER 14

## *velociraptor snacks*

The first unusual thing that Eric noticed was an increase in the number of ancestors. At first, he thought they had come to gawk at the visitors, but no one seemed interested in Eric and Rose. They were all in a hurry and barely had time to answer the guard's questions. Weet had been gone for about an hour and Eric and Rose had spent most of the time in worried silence.

"What's happening?" asked Rose, "Are they coming to get us?"

"No," replied Eric, "they don't seem interested in us. They're all heading towards the river."

The children edged out of the shelter to watch. The guards, busy with the people rushing by, paid them no attention. Eric and Rose watched in confusion, both wishing that Weet were still with them. Intent on their observations, they moved to within a few feet of the guards. Neither of them noticed the velociraptor until the guard on the right collapsed screaming beneath a deadly feathered body. Instinctively, Eric jumped backwards, knocking Rose over in the process. This saved his life. A second velociraptor, a fraction slower than the first, dropped onto the space where he had just been standing. Pandemonium erupted. Ancestors were running everywhere, whistling in fear and jostling for ladders and creepers. More and more velociraptors were dropping through the branches all the time.

"Smart," flashed through Eric's mind, "attacking from above."

The velociraptor in front of him was recovering from the surprise of missing its target. It would not miss the second time. Pushing Rose behind him, Eric grabbed the club from the felled guard. More top heavy than the softball bats he was used to, it still reminded him of stepping up to home plate. The velociraptor leapt. Eric swung with all his might. The arc of the swing ended with a loud crack. The velociraptor dropped like a loosely-filled sack and lay still.

"Home run," thought Eric.

Holding the club in front of him, he retreated under the canopy where Rose huddled with Sally and Sinor. The second guard was still on his feet swinging his club, but he was in the centre of four attackers who knew enough to keep out of range. It would only be a matter of time. Eric was debating going to his assistance when one of the attackers leapt. The club swung, but it had been a feint. The real attack came from behind. Soon the guard was down and the velociraptors were busy feeding.

"Quick!" Eric pushed Rose and the two pets through the hole at the back of the shelter that Weet had used.

There were no creatures in sight behind the shelter, only a rickety ladder leading up into the branches.

"That's the way we go," said Eric, tucking the club under his arm. "We have to get up above the velociraptors."

Fortunately, the ladder was sturdier than it looked and the rungs were quite wide. It was also angled, which freed Eric's hands to help the others. Sally had to be carried, but she kept still tucked under Eric's arm. Rose was silent and looked very frightened, but she managed on her own and Sinor was remarkably adept, needing no assistance as he jumped lightly to the upper levels.

As they climbed, the ladders became shorter and the platforms between them smaller. They began to pass small shelters which were obviously the ancestors' living quarters. Sleeping mats were everywhere and many had plates of fruit and dried fish beside them, but there was no sign of life.

At last, they could go no higher. They were on a

small platform surrounded by dense foliage. The cramped shelter in one corner looked as though it had not been occupied for some time. Exhausted with the climb, the small party collapsed into it. Rose was the first to recover enough to speak.

"What happened?" she asked in a frightened voice. "I thought those things couldn't climb trees."

"So did I," replied Eric, still breathless, "but apparently they have learned. Those things are smart. That was a planned attack; an ambush from above. They must be all through the city—that would explain the ancestors heading for the river."

"I hate this place!" Rose was almost in tears. "I wish we were back home."

Eric did too, but he was as terrified of what they might find there as he was of the velociraptors below.

"At least we're safe for now," he tried to comfort her.

"This isn't like the last time." Rose's tears were coming freely now. "Where's Weet? How will he ever find us? How will we ever escape? I hate those things."

Eric hugged his sister as she sobbed against his chest. He was close to tears himself, but having to comfort Rose kept him from breaking down himself.

"I don't know how Weet will do it," he said honestly when Rose had calmed a little, "but I'm sure he'll find us and we'll get out of this mess."

The words sounded convincing, but Eric wasn't sure he believed them. What if he and Rose had been killed in the car crash? Did that mean that even though they had time-jumped, they were destined to die here too? If they were dead in the other world, obviously they couldn't go back. Perhaps he should tell Rose the truth about the crash.

He never had a chance to make up his mind. A rustling below them caused Sally to prick up her ears. She had been lying in front of the shelter and now crawled over and peered down. What she saw made her burst into frantic barking. Eric disentangled himself from Rose, picked up the club and crawled to join his dog. For a moment, he hoped somehow it might be Weet, but Sally sounded very angry. Looking over the edge he saw why. On the platform below, less than ten feet down, was a pack of eight velociraptors. They were sniffing the air and looking up at him. One was cautiously beginning to climb the sloping ladder. The beast was a little awkward, but was making steady progress.

"What is it?" Rose was behind Eric.

"Velociraptors," Eric replied in a whisper. "But it's all right. As long as they can only come up the ladder, we can pick them off one by one."

The first velociraptor's head was almost level with the platform. Eric swung. There was a crack, and the creature disappeared from sight. Eric looked over to

see it lying twitching on the level below. Through his fear, he felt elated. This was simple. No secrets he couldn't tell, just the swing of the club to defend himself and his party. He could do this all day.

The next velociraptor was beginning its climb. Eric drew back and tensed, club ready. As the head appeared he swung. The head vanished. Then, before he could swing again, it reappeared, followed by the feathered body.

"It ducked!" he thought in amazement as the beast landed on the platform beside him. Unfortunately for the velociraptor, it landed too close to Eric. His return swing caught it on the side before it could launch an attack. The blow sent the creature sliding off the platform to crash down through the small branches.

But now there was a third one on the platform, and this one stayed just out of range of the club and gazed at Eric with a pair of pale, cold eyes. Its purpose was not to attack, but to protect the top of the ladder. Already, Eric could see the next head. He stepped forward, just as the second velociraptor jumped up.

Now there were two facing Eric's club and they were far enough apart that he could only focus on one at a time. With a sinking heart he chose the one on the right, keeping in mind the feint attack he had seen before. As he swung, he could almost feel the claws of the other attacker at his side. Somehow he stayed focused enough to drive his target off the platform despite an awareness of activity on his left.

"Strike three," he thought as the creature fell from view. Turning to face the other threat, he was amazed to see the creature wearing a Royal Tyrrell Museum of Palaeontology sweatshirt. The shirt was covering the beast's head and its foreclaws were scrabbling to tear it off.

They never got a chance. With a very satisfying crack, velociraptor and sweatshirt disappeared over the edge. Rose was jumping up and down in agitated excitement. "Got it! Got it!" she was shouting.

The next velociraptor had reached the platform, but it was alone and hesitant. It watched Eric closely as he moved in for a blow. The velociraptor was so focused on Eric that it never saw Sinor and Sally, charging from opposite sides. Sinor hit first and the beast staggered. Then came Sally and it toppled, surprised, over the edge.

No more velociraptors climbed up. Eric crawled over and peered down. The three uninjured survivors were looking back up at him and one other animal lay twitching beside them. They looked as if they were trying to decide what to do next. Eventually, they squatted down in a semi-circle, alternately watching their injured companion and the ladder.

"Well, it doesn't look like they're going to attack again," said Eric, "but one of us will have to keep an eye on them all the time." How they would do that after night fell was a problem to which Eric had no solution as yet.

"That sweatshirt trick was great!" he praised Rose. He felt elated. He had been scared, really scared, but for the moment they had won.

"Yeah, we showed them," Rose responded happily. "How many are still down there?"

"Three," Eric replied, "and one wounded one. They just seem to be sitting there. We can handle them if they try and come up."

"Yes," agreed Rose, "but we can't stay here forever. What are we going to do?"

Eric had no answer. "I don't know," he said honestly. "Perhaps they'll get tired of waiting and go away." It seemed like a slim hope and Eric had trouble seeing how it would help them anyway, they had nowhere to go. Both children lapsed into silence as they lay and watched their attackers.

The sense of triumph was rapidly vanishing as they began to think about their position. They were stuck without food or any way of escape. It was probably only a matter of time before other velociraptors found them. Already, it was late afternoon. Fear of the coming night crept into Eric's mind. It was interrupted by Rose.

"Look," she said, pointing down, "one of them is sick."

Eric looked down. One of the three velociraptors did indeed appear to be unwell. It was up on its hind legs, staggering around emitting hoarse coughing noises. Its companions watched it impassively. If it stumbled too close, they hissed a warning at it, but it paid no attention. Several times it fell. At last it did not seem to have the strength to rise again and lay twitching on the platform. What was happening? Was it a trick? Eric doubted it. The creature really did look sick.

Nothing much happened for some time. The light was already beginning to fade when the two remaining velociraptors rose. They crossed to the bottom of the ladder. Eric tensed.

"Here we go again," he said, clutching the club tighter. But the animals made no attempt to climb. For a few moments they stood looking up and then, without even a second glance at their fallen comrades, departed through the branches.

"What's going on?" Rose sounded tense. "Why are they leaving? Is it a trick?"

"I don't know," Eric replied thoughtfully, "If it is, it's very elaborate. I don't think so. Why would they leave? They have us trapped, and they just need to wait until dark. They don't know we don't have any food or water up here."

"OK," Rose pondered, "if it's not a trick, what do we do now?'

"Well," replied Eric, thinking as he spoke, "we'll wait till the moon comes up. That will give us some light. Then we'll try and find our way down to the river. Weet said there were outcasts on an island. Maybe we can find a boat and get to them."

It sounded like a risky plan. The thought of finding their way through the velociraptor-infested tree city was not inviting, but Eric could think of nothing else. They certainly couldn't stay here.

"I wish Weet was here," Rose said wistfully, "he would know what to do." Eric was a little offended at the suggestion that he didn't know what to do, but he decided to let it slide. After all, he felt the same way too.

"Rose," he said after awhile, "there's something I want to tell you, just in case . . ."

"What?" Rose peered at him in the failing light.

"The car crash . . . that sent us here," Eric hesitated. Rose had to know in case they went back suddenly or she alone returned to their world. "It was worse than I said."

Rose looked at him quizzically. This was hard. Swallowing, he continued, "The truck hit us very hard."

"What do you mean?"

"Well," he continued, "I think we must all have been hurt very badly."

"But we're fine," Rose looked down at herself. This wasn't getting any easier.

"Yes," said Eric, "but I think we time-jumped at the last minute. I think we might have been killed in the real world."

Rose looked at him. "Mom and Dad?" she asked.

"Yes," said Eric. He was ready for Rose's tears, but not her reply.

"That's nonsense," Rose said confidently. Eric peered at her. "This isn't heaven. We're not dead, and neither are Mom and Dad. Don't be silly, Eric. Anyway, when we go back, we'll arrive before we left, just like last time, and we can tell Dad to pull over and the truck will miss us. Now come on, the moon's out and we should be going to the river to find Weet."

Stunned, Eric watched the shadowy shape of his sister as she got herself ready to descend. He would never understand her, but how he wished for her certainty. Picking up Sally, he lowered himself over the edge into the darkness.

# CHAPTER 15

## on the river

**P**oor things!" Eric looked at his sister in amazement. Those "poor things" had been trying to kill them both just a short while before. There was no explaining Rose.

In full moonlight, the foursome retraced their steps to the morning shelter. Thankfully, they had not seen any velociraptors, at least not any live ones. Several of the platforms they had crossed had been occupied by velociraptor bodies. Eric had stumbled over the first one and it had given him quite a start, but it had been dead for some time. So had the others they had seen. None of them appeared injured and there was no sign of any fighting around the bodies. Eric couldn't work it out, but he was certainly glad they weren't alive. The one in front of them now was alive, but it was in obvious distress. It was coughing and staggering about like the one they had seen in the afternoon.

"It's just like that poor shovelbill we saw in Weet's country," Rose continued. A switch clicked in Eric's brain.

"Of course!" he exclaimed. "The sickness."

"What do you mean?" Rose whispered, although there wasn't anyone around to overhear her.

"The sickness that was killing the shovelbills at Weet's home," Eric continued as the pieces fell into place in his brain. "Weet said that the sick animals had more of those parasites on them. They must be what carried the disease."

"So?" Rose was impatient with long explanations.

"The maiasaura we rode over the mountains on had the parasites too . . ."

"Why didn't it die?" Rose interrupted, eager to find a flaw with her brother's thesis.

"I'm not sure," answered Eric. "Perhaps there has to be a heavy infestation to kill a large animal or maybe some of the shovelbills are immune. In any case, the velociraptors ate the maiasaura. They got the sickness. Weet said the parasites breed very quickly. If the velociraptors had no immunity to the sickness, it would spread through them like wildfire."

As if to confirm his theory, the velociraptor in front of them gave a harsh cough and keeled over to lie twitching on the mat. Eric was feeling good. The velociraptors seemed less of a threat now. They were not invincible. The bugs and Eric's club could take care of them.

His growing feeling of security was dashed by a low growl from Sally. It was accompanied by a rustling in the branches behind him. Turning, he raised his club. He was relieved to see that the figure emerging from the darkness wasn't a velociraptor. For a moment he hoped it might be Weet, but the moonlight glinting off the shells told him otherwise.

The old shell seller from the market stepped forward. Ignoring Sally's warning growls, he walked up to Eric and performed the cupped hands greeting. Eric responded in kind. Then, with a half-beckoning gesture, the old ancestor moved off through the shadows.

"Where's he going?" Rose sounded panicky.

"I don't know," replied Eric, "but I guess we should follow him. At least he knows his way around here."

Keeping as much as possible to the deeper shadows, the small group made their way back to the now deserted open platform. Without a sound, their guide clambered over the edge. By the time Eric got there, the ancestor was several rungs down a ladder made of knotted creepers. By now, Eric was quite adept at ladders, but this one stretched vertically down three stories to the river bank. It was a journey he would not have relished in broad daylight. To attempt it with a dog clutched under his arm and in the middle of the night smacked of insanity. Apparently, Rose shared his opinion.

"I'm not going down there," she breathed urgently in his ear.

Despite his obviously advanced years and the encumbrance of a large collection of shells, their guide was making remarkable progress. As they watched, he reached the bottom. Without even looking up, he moved to one side and began fiddling with some creepers. In a flash, he had disentangled one and was hauling on it vigorously. A few seconds later a sturdy basket was sitting beside them on the platform.

"Of course," Eric breathed, relaxing a little, "they must have a system for bringing up supplies, taking down fishing equipment or whatever they need down there. We can lower Sally and Sinor in the basket."

"And me too," Rose added hurriedly. "I'm not going down that ladder."

Rose, Sally and Sinor were ferried down one by one while Eric made his cautious way down the ladder. It felt good to Eric to have solid ground beneath his feet once more, but he couldn't help searching the shadows for any suspicious movement of mottled feathers. Beyond the water's edge, the river gleamed in the silver moonlight as it flew past with frightening speed.

As soon as they were all down, the guide indicated a wide canoe-like boat beached nearby. It was made of what appeared to be tree bark stretched over a framework of curved branches. Several sleek paddles lay inside. The boat was surprisingly light, but only with considerable effort did they manage to manoeuvre it into the water. Using hand signs, the guide warned them to step only on the branches forming the ribs. While he held the end steady, Eric helped Rose in and lifted Sally and Sinor over the edge. At intervals along the length of the boat, flatter pieces of wood formed rough seats.

They had only just settled onto the seats when the old man stepped nimbly into the boat and pushed off. Instantly, the current grasped the craft and swept it away from the shore. Rose gasped as they spun around and the old guide struggled to regain control. Eventually, they stabilized near the middle of the current. They were pointing downstream and all except the guide were facing backwards. He steered using a broad paddle which fitted into a notch on the boat's stern.

Perched uncomfortably in the middle of the boat, Eric considered the moonlight a mixed blessing. On the one hand, it enabled them to see where they were going and avoid major obstacles. On the other, in gave a ghostly view of the distant trees racing past at an unsettling speed.

Despite the worrying scene, Eric found he was almost mesmerized by the passing shapes. As his eyes became more accustomed to the gloom, he began to pick out more detail. The scene was not nearly as empty as he had first imagined. Dark, moving shapes were quite common on the wide sandy banks. Some appeared to have the sinuous shape of crocodiles while others seemed bulky and turtle-like. The air, too, was alive and a variety of flying creatures flashed rapidly across Eric's field of vision. High-pitched squeaks suggested that at least some of them were bats.

After half an hour of racing down the river, Eric began to feel quite comfortable. Their speed seemed to have slowed a little and there appeared to be little threat from either the river or its inhabitants. In fact, the river banks fell away as the river widened. Soon they were in open water and could feel the distinctive rise and fall of an ocean swell beneath the canoe. Looking over his shoulder, Eric could see a dark shape ahead.

"We're heading for that island," he informed Rose. "I wonder if that's where the outcasts live." He got no response from his sister. She was sitting in a huddle, looking obviously unwell. The sickness! Eric felt panic rising. "Rose . . . " he began. Rose looked up. In the pale moonlight she looked ghostly.

"I'm going to . . . " she began, but she got no farther. With a lurch that shook the whole canoe, she grabbed the side and stuck her head over the edge. Eric could hear retching sounds. He relaxed. Rose was the world's worst sailor. Her stomach became queasy on ferry rides to Vancouver Island. Eric laughed with relief.

Rose pulled her pale face back into the canoe.

"What's so funny?" she asked weakly.

"Nothing," replied Eric hurriedly, "I just thought for a minute you had the sickness."

"I'm not a velociraptor," Rose responded as she slumped back into a miserable pile at the bottom of the canoe.

Eric reckoned the time to be close to midnight when the canoe bumped gently onto the island's sandy beach. He was exhausted, hungry and thirsty. Rose was asleep. The old shell-seller jumped out and hauled the canoe up the beach. Sinor was the first out, bounding around on the sand. Eric lifted Sally down and the two animals soon disappeared towards the trees. Gently, the old guide lifted Rose out onto the sand where she stood groggily. Eric joined them.

As they moved up the beach, Eric made out dark shapes near the trees. Sally and Sinor's joyful leaps told him the identity of one of them.

"Weet!" he said. "It's Weet!" Rose looked up. A figure was running toward them now. Soon the three figures were locked in an embrace.

"Oh, Weet!" was all Rose could manage before he swept her off her feet and carried her up the beach. Eric followed as they entered the trees and found themselves in a large sleeping circle. A dozen figures sat around a central fire which had died down to a dull glow.

"A fire," said Eric.

"Yes," Weet said proudly to his friend, "I make."

Quickly the fire was built up until it gave a healthy light. Food and water were brought and the visitors ate their fill. Eric couldn't remember food which tasted any better. The only problem was that he couldn't keep his eyes open. Already Rose was asleep, curled on a mat by the fire.

"What happened at the city?" he asked, but he never heard a reply. He was asleep before Weet could think of the right word to begin with.

Weet was very happy. He had been sure that Eric, Rose, Sa"y and Sinor had been caught by the sickleclaws, but now here they were, tired but all in one piece. He looked forward to hearing their story. Gently he stepped over Eric's sleeping form and lay down on his own mat. It had been quite a day. He was wondering what tomorrow would bring when he felt a hand stretch over from the mat next to his. Gently he took it in his own. "Saar," he whistled softly, then in Eric's strange language, "good night."

# CHAPTER 16

*return*

**D**appled sunlight penetrated the leaves when Eric awoke to find Rose sitting up beside him eating a nan and looking a lot better than she had in the canoe the night before. She had always needed less sleep than him.

"About time, sleepy head," she said as he sat up.

"Good morning to you too," Eric replied as he looked around. A little way off, Sally and Sinor were sitting on an untidy pile of brush. Weet and Saar sat beside the glowing remains of the fire. Other ancestors were scattered around the clearing, eating, tidying the sleeping mats or whistling softly.

"Good morning," said Eric, looking at Weet.

"Good morning," repeated Weet and Saar in unison. "Sleep good?" Weet asked as he passed Eric some fruit.

"Yes, thank you," Eric replied. "Where are we? Are these the outcasts?" he added.

Weet paused long enough to make Eric think he hadn't heard the question before replying: "Outcasts.

Yes. And some from city." Weet made a sweeping gesture with his arm.

Following the arc with his eyes, Eric noticed other figures through the trees and other sleeping circles. The old shell-seller was sitting across the fire watching them.

"Who is he?" Rose indicated their shell-covered guide.

"He is Saar's father," explained Weet. "His name is Soron. He is . . . son, son, son, son, son of first Weet."

"Wow," said Eric. Then a thought struck him.

"So you and he are very distantly related. The first Weet was your common ancestor."

Weet nodded.

"This is all beginning to make some sense," Eric continued. "And who better to keep in contact with the outcasts than a shell collector and seller who has to go out on long collecting expeditions?"

Another question crossed his mind.

"What happened in the city?"

Weet was again silent as he searched for words. Then he slowly told the story.

After Weet and Saar had left Eric and Rose, they had gone to a meeting high in the trees. There had been many ancestors there, including Soron, and they had been planning an escape from the city that night to join the outcasts. There had been much discussion about how they would manage to take

Eric and Rose, and what their prospects would be in the long term if they joined the outcasts. But the discussion had become pointless when the velociraptors had attacked.

Apparently, the beasts had attacked by the hundreds in a well coordinated assault. At four or five places throughout the city, velociraptors had piled themselves up against the lower part of the tree trunks. Many of them had died in the crush, but their sacrifice had enabled many others to climb over their bodies and reach the lowest platforms. Once in the trees, they had spread rapidly through the city's thoroughfares, killing as they went. There had been little time to organize resistance and they had overrun most of the city very quickly.

Weet and Saar's group, on an upper level, had only been able to watch in horror as the velociraptors swept through the trees below them. Weet's whistling had kept the attackers at bay, but it was not enough to repel the invasion. However, Weet had felt confident enough of his whistling skills to lead a reconnaissance trip. He and Saar had witnessed Seel, Sam and Saura leading a last stand on the communal meeting platform. It had been brave, but it had also been useless.

Many of the ancestors had thrown themselves over the edge into the river rather than face the inevitable claws. Saar could only hope that a few of them had managed to reach safety. By mid-afternoon, only a few pockets of ancestors had remained, like Eric and Rose, on isolated high platforms. Their prospects were not great. The velociraptors could not reach them but, unless they could get down, they faced lingering starvation.

Weet and Saar had assembled as many of the diverse groups as they could and armed them with whatever weapons they could find. Their only hope had been to escape the city and try to meet up with the outcasts. They had to fight hard at first, but, aided by Weet's whistling, they had made progress. Gradually, they had noticed that the velociraptors were beginning to withdraw and were leaving only sick ones behind. By dusk, the survivors had made it to the river and paddled for the island of the outcasts.

Weet had been determined to stay and look for his friends, but Soron had volunteered to remain and look for them. He was a much better choice for the job since he knew every secret route in the city like the back of his own hand.

When Weet had finished, Eric explained his theory about the sickness being brought by the bugs on the maiasaura. Weet nodded. It made sense.

"What will we do now?" Rose was ever practical.

"Ancestors go back city," Weet explained. That made sense too if the sickleclaws were all dead or at least weak enough that they could be driven away. The ancestors might even move down from the trees to return to living as they had before the sickleclaws arrived.

"And what about the outcasts?" Eric continued. "Will they go back to the city too?"

Weet looked at Saar. "Some," he said. "Others go Fire Mountain."

"And you will lead them, just like your ancestor." It was as much a statement as a question.

Weet and Saar both nodded.

"Then we will come too," Rose said determinedly. In any case, there was little choice. Weet was their security, their interpreter and their talisman in this world. But Eric felt sad. The way Weet had looked at Saar made him feel excluded and lonely. He felt that he had lost Weet. During the few days of their journey over the mountains, all three of them had become very close, but Eric had somehow felt that he was developing a strong, special friendship with Weet. Now, Weet's closeness to Saar seemed to loosen that bond. He felt close to tears.

"I'm going to check out the beach," he said as lightly as he could.

The sight over the water almost made him forget his troubles. The vast desert of sand they had crossed after their landing last night was gone. In its place, sparkling blue water rolled gently past.

To his right he could see the dark line of the mainland and the lighter blue of the river mouth. To his left, several dark green islands broke the surface of the sea.

It was a view worthy of any calendar, but it was the view's inhabitants that really caught Eric's attention. The air and water seemed to be alive with every kind of flying and swimming creature imaginable. White dots blanketed the water in places and swirled in apparently aimless flight across the sky. To Eric, the closest ones looked like seagulls, except for their large red and yellow beaks.

Several kinds of variously coloured ducks paddled placidly on the surface or dived for fish. One, the size of a swan, was entirely black except for an orange beak perched on the end of an incredibly long neck. Most of the time it floated completely still until it spotted prey. Then the neck arched gracefully down and the bird, powered by strong webbed orange feet, disappeared in pursuit. Upon surfacing the creature gulped down its wriggling, silvery catch. Then it pushed itself out of the water and flapped two stubby wings which were obviously no use for anything remotely resembling flight.

The most dramatic flyers were in the distance and reminded Eric of his first moments in this world. Pteranodons, ranging in size from sea gull to Cessna, glided effortlessly above the water, without so much as a hesitation in their flight, dipping their long necks occasionally to dredge up a protesting fish.

A commotion among the floating birds caught Eric's attention. Amidst a flurry of wings, about half-a-dozen snake-like necks emerged from the depths. They reached close to ten feet above the water before arching back under the surface to be followed by a humped back and short stubby tail.

"Plesiosaurs," Eric gasped in amazement.

"What?" Rose and Sally had joined him.

"Plesiosaurs," repeated her brother. "Loch Ness monsters."

Rose gazed in wonder at the scene before her.

"Great place for a cottage," said Eric, "but I don't know if I'd like to go swimming in that sea."

Rose nodded as she watched the strange scene before her. "Eric, do you think we'll ever get home?"

Eric was unprepared for the question. "I don't know," he replied honestly. "It all seems so random. We could be sent back at any moment, or not at all."

"We have to get back," said Rose quietly. "We have to stop the accident from happening."

"Yes," agreed Eric wistfully, "but I don't see how we can have any control over what happens. Perhaps if we return over the mountains we can find the tree where the Tyrannosaurus attacked us or the collapsed tunnel where we first came through. That might give us a clue."

It didn't seem like much to hope for, but it was all he could think of. Rose nodded silently. After a moment Eric continued.

"In any case, I think we should tell Weet what will happen to his world. He came all this way to find out what the ancestors could tell him and he's no further ahead."

"He found Saar," interrupted Rose, always the romantic.

"Yes," agreed Eric as his sadness at having lost his friend flooded back. "I think they both deserve to know the truth. I thought it would be simple coming back here and meeting Weet again, but it's just as complicated as our world."

Rose wasn't listening. She was gazing up into the bright blue sky.

"Look, a shooting star!" she said. Eric looked up. You didn't get shooting stars in broad daylight! But there it was, curving across the sky, a line of fire. Eric shivered as he remembered the meteor he had seen so long before amongst the hoodoos. But this one wasn't alone—the whole sky was crisscrossed with long, curving, fiery trails. The blue of the sky was being painted orange and red as thousands of lumps of cold rock flared on their journey through the Earth's atmosphere.

"It's a meteor shower," gasped Eric in amazement, "and a big one if we can see it in daylight!"

The first one curved down and disappeared over the horizon. The next one splashed down in a column of steam amongst the plesiosaurs.

"What?" was all he had time to shout as more columns of steam rose from the sea before him. Sea birds took flight in panic. Meteorites were churning the water into white foam beneath a cloud of steam. A loud, dull thunk, told him that one had landed somewhere close by. As Eric looked down the narrow strip of beach, a crater about six feet across appeared in a cloud of sand uncomfortably close to them.

"Quick," he said, grabbing Rose's hand and turning back towards their sleeping circle. A loud roar and the sound of ripping vegetation indicated the passage of a meteorite through the branches above their heads. The scene before Eric was one of absolute chaos. Figures were running in all directions, stumbling over fallen branches and over each other. Meteorites were whipping through the trees above their heads, making loud cracks whenever they hit a trunk or large branch. Weet and Saar were standing arm in arm by the fire looking back at Eric and Rose. Weet had his free arm outstretched towards his friend.

"This is it . . ." thought Eric, and then aloud, "come on!"

Pulling on Rose's hand, Eric headed for Weet. It

was no safer over there, but if this was the end of the world, Eric wanted to be beside his friend. He had taken precisely three steps when a particularly loud roar ended in a blast of hot air and a deafening crash. Sand, leaves and bits of branch were flung violently in his face. His momentum carried him forward for one more step. It was a step into nothingness. Eric felt himself falling. He was still holding Rose's hand and he could feel Sally at his feet. Someone was screaming. Maybe it was himself. He kept falling, falling forever into a hot, woolly blackness. Then everything went quiet.

# CHAPTER 17

### changing the future

The first thing Eric was aware of was his father's voice, "Not too long now. We've made good time. Another hour or so should get us to Kamloops. Keep an eye out for a motel."

Eric was confused. Where was he? Through the windows he could see dark trees and a crumbling rock wall. He had a vague sense of being somewhere he shouldn't be, and there was something important he had to do. But what?

"I'm hungry, when are we going to eat?" said a voice from the seat beside him.

"As soon as we get to Kamloops," his mother replied, "we'll find a restaurant and have supper."

What was it he was trying to remember? He had been in danger. There was a beach and someone had been throwing stones in the water.

"But I'm hungry now. I can't wait another hour." Rose was beginning to whine.

Eric remembered running, or at least trying to. Had something been chasing him? This was annoying. What was he supposed to remember? He shook his head to try and clear it. Outside the rock wall raced past in a blur of speed. Eric had a sense of being on a roller coaster heading for somewhere, but with no power to slow down or change direction.

"Rose, we're going as fast as we can. If you're really hungry have a piece of fruit from the bag."

Rose leant forward and picked something out of a bag at her feet. She took a bite.

"Yecch, it's sour," she said, dropping the apple back on the floor.

"Pick it up please."

Weet! The velociraptors. The meteor storm. The outcasts. Everything rushed back to him in a flash. His memories were just as vivid as from his first visit. Not a dream, but a journey in time. He remembered it all. No, not all. There was something still nagging at the back of his mind. Something he couldn't quite recall. Something he had to do. Did Rose remember this time? Eric looked over at his sister, gazing out the car window.

"Rose," he whispered, "do you remember?"

"What?" Rose looked confused. "Remember what?"

Eric hesitated. He didn't want to have his memories denied again. The thought of being alone with his experiences was frightening, but he had to find out what it was he couldn't quite remember. Somehow, he knew it was important.

"Weet," he said slowly.

A puzzled look crossed his sister's face. "Weet?" she said tentatively. Eric's heart leapt. Maybe she would remember this time. "I'm not sure."

Eric tried again, "Saar. The tree city. The meteorites. The outcasts." Rose's brow furrowed in concentration. Eric had to find something else to jog her memory. What was the most vivid thing that had happened to them in Weet's time? "The velociraptors, remember, we were trapped and they were climbing up. We had to fight them."

Rose opened her mouth as if to say something.

"Rose, where's your sweatshirt? I hope it's not crumpled up on the floor somewhere." Their mother was still on the tidiness theme. Rose looked up.

"I threw it over the . . ."

"What?" interrupted her mother and Eric in unison. Rose glanced at Eric, then back to her mother. "I don't know Mom. I guess it's around somewhere. Sorry, I'll look for it when we stop."

"OK," their mother said, "but do try to be more careful with your stuff."

Rose looked at her brother. "I threw it over that horrible thing with feathers and then you hit it," she said quietly.

Eric felt like cheering. He wasn't alone any more. "Do you remember it all?" he asked.

"I think so," Rose was concentrating. "We

travelled over some hills, past a volcano, and there was the city with the veloci…things. Was it a dream?"

"No," said Eric firmly. "How could it be if we both remember? And where is your sweatshirt?"

Rose shook her head. "What happened to Weet? I remember an explosion."

"There was a meteorite shower at the outcasts' island. They were landing all around us. I guess a large one landed close by. I remember falling, maybe into a crater."

"But is Weet OK?" Rose interrupted.

"I don't know," was all Eric could say. If it was just a local shower, like the fire nights Weet had mentioned, then he might be all right. If it was part of the big one that ended the dinosaurs' reign, then he wouldn't be.

"But Rose," Eric continued, "there's something else. Something that's important but I can't remember what." Ahead of the car, a glow appeared from a set of very large headlights. The wrinkle appeared again on Rose's forehead. She glanced out the windscreen at the approaching light. Then she went very still.

"Eric, the crash!" she said.

A chill swept down Eric's spine. Suddenly, his memories of Weet's world dissolved in the urgency of this one. Bolt upright, he gazed through the front windshield. There was a definite glow ahead and it was getting brighter.

"Pull over Dad!" Eric had said it without even thinking.

"What?" his father replied. "We'll be in Kamloops soon and we can stop then, have something to eat and get a good rest."

The glow was headlights, bright ones. In a moment they would be around the bend and then it would be too late. He had to do something to avoid the horrible shattering, screaming protest of the accident. But what?

"I'm going to throw up," Rose yelled. Their mother half turned, "Are you feeling sick?" she demanded.

"Yes, she is," Eric was shouting now too, "and so am I. We have to stop!"

"Pull over!" Eric's Mom's voice was added to the chorus.

"There's not much room this close to a corner," Eric's Dad wasn't stopping. "Can you wait a minute?"

The headlights were visible now, frighteningly close to Eric's panic stricken mind.

"It's urgent!" Rose screamed. Eric jammed his fingers down his throat and retched convincingly. Sally began to bark. The car was slowing now. Eric could hear the sound of the gravel shoulder under the wheels.

The lights were almost on them and the car's interior was bathed in their unearthly harshness.

"He's on the wrong side!" gasped their mother.

"Move over," Eric's Dad yelled at the approaching danger. The car jerked and skidded as he stood on the brakes. The air was filled with the booming sound of the truck's air horn. The car lurched as the back wheels caught the edge of the ditch. It shuddered as if the thundering truck were trying to suck it back out onto the road. Then, almost miraculously, they were bathed in silence. It was broken only by the release of the breath no one realized they had been holding. For a long moment no one spoke. It was Eric's Dad who finally broke the silence.

"The idiot," he growled, his hands gripping the steering wheel, "he could have killed us!"

Eric was salivating uncontrollably from his attempts to throw up. He could feel saliva trickling down his chin. Lifting his arm to wipe it away, he noticed that his hand was shaking. Reaching down, he pulled Sally close to him and buried his hands in her warm coat.

"Are you all right?" his mother asked.

All right? Eric didn't know. They were all still alive, and he was glad about that. He was confused by the sudden dislocation from one world to the other and saddened by the loss of Weet. Nothing was simple, not in this world or Weet's. Wishing for another life wasn't going to make it so, it merely changed the problems. Like it or not, Eric was going to have to get on with life in his own world.

"Do you still feel like throwing up?" His mother was still concerned.

"No," Eric managed to whisper, "I'm all right now." At least he wasn't alone. Rose remembered. They were in this thing together. Eric turned to his sister who sat beside him looking as stunned as everyone else.

"Welcome back, Rose," he said and gave her a big hug.

photo by Tom Shardlow

## About the Author

John Wilson lives on Vancouver Island. After a life as a geologist in Scotland, Zimbabwe and Alberta, John began writing in 1989. His freelance work and poetry have appeared in many newspapers and magazines and his children's stories in Chickadee. His other books for young people are the novel *Weet,* which begins the adventures of Eric, Rose and Sally, and *Across Frozen Seas,* an historical fiction based around the lost Franklin expedition to the Canadian Arctic in 1845.